Heart, Haunt, Havoc

The Gideon Testaments Book One
Freydís Moon

TIPTON CO. LIBRARY
TIPTON, INDIANA

Also by Freydís ☽

Exodus 20:3
With A Vengeance
Three Kings

The Gideon Testaments
Heart, Haunt, Havoc
Wolf, Willow, Witch
Saint, Sorrow, Sinner

Praise For ☽

Olivia Waite named *Heart, Haunt, Havoc* a New York Times Best Romance Book of 2023

"Eerie as a haunting, biting as the midwinter night, and as tender as the ache of new love, *Heart, Haunt, Havoc* lingers long past the last page."
—**K. M. Enright** author of *Mistress of Lies*

"[*Heart, Haunt, Havoc* is] filled with dark magic, romance, and high stakes, this is a fast-paced read that pulls you through to the dramatic conclusion and doesn't disappoint!"
—**C. M. Rosens** author of *The Crows*

"Masterful! Moon has an expert understanding of characters and unique voices. *The Gideon Testaments* is [an] emotional, queer triumph..."
—**Lucien Burr** author of *The Teras Trials*

CONTENT NOTE

Heart, Haunt, Havoc contains sensitive material, including but not limited to: sexual content, body horror, animal death (and resurrection), horror, depiction of dysphoria, murder, graverobbing, discussion of racism, gore

BUT DAMN IF THERE ISN'T ANYTHING SEXIER
THAN A SLENDER BOY WITH A HANDGUN,
A FAST CAR, A BOTTLE OF PILLS.
WHAT WOULD YOU LIKE? I'D LIKE MY MONEY'S WORTH.
TRY EXPLAINING A LIFE BUNDLED WITH EPISODES OF THIS—
SWALLOWING MUD, SWALLOWING GLASS, THE SMELL OF BLOOD
ON THE FIRST FOUR KNUCKLES.

WE PULL OUR BOOTS ON WITH BOTH HANDS
BUT WE CAN'T PUNCH OURSELVES AWAKE AND ALL I CAN DO
IS STAND ON THE CURB AND SAY SORRY
ABOUT THE BLOOD IN YOUR MOUTH. I WISH IT WAS MINE.

I COULDN'T GET THE BOY TO KILL ME
BUT I WORE HIS JACKET FOR THE LONGEST TIME.

Richard Siken

CHAPTER ONE

THE HOUSE ON STAGHORN WAY appeared extraordinarily normal. The stark white shutters wore a fresh coat of paint and Colin Hart's polished shoes made hollow, hooflike sounds on the sturdy, renovated porch. Unlike his typical business engagements, this particular house refused to breathe. Instead, it stayed entirely still, as if the bones that held its two floors, five rooms, and single occupier had gone brittle the moment an exorcist arrived.

Well, not an exorcist, exactly. A *specialist*, maybe. Someone used to the way a house wheezed and bent, watched and wondered. Someone who knocked precisely four times, and adjusted the high collar on his tweed coat, clutching a briefcase in leather-clad fingers. Someone who knew how to strike a smile as the door floated open, even when ice dropped like an anchor into his stomach.

"Bishop, I assume? Bishop Martínez?" Colin said, focusing on the slight, neatly dressed person standing in the doorway, and not on the strangely shaped body—skeletal, bruised, and curious—lingering over their shoulder at the top of the staircase. "I'm Mr. Hart."

Bishop adjusted the square reading glasses perched on their handsome, hawkish nose, and nodded curtly. "Hi, yeah, that's me." They paused, scanning Colin from his onyx Chelsea boots to his high, round, freckled cheeks. "Oh, right—come in. Sorry, I . . . I'm not used to actually *inviting* people inside. It's been—"

"Inconvenient, I assume?" Colin stepped onto the cherrywood floor and watched the apparition peering at them from the second story wink out of existence. "Tell me about the house . . ." He turned his gaze to Bishop. "Do you prefer *mx* or *mister* or . . . ?"

"Bishop is fine, actually. They, them."

Colin lifted an eyebrow. "He, him for me, thank you. If we're embracing informality, call me Colin." He glanced at the ceiling, then the floor. "So, the house."

Bishop closed the door and turned the lock, smoothing delicate hands over the front of their maroon long-sleeve. Colin took a moment to study the homeowner's sturdy jaw and fine, tightened mouth. Bishop's eyelashes flicked, chasing shadows along their cheekbones, and they straightened their narrow shoulders, aligning themself toward the decorative banister. *Gentle*, Colin thought, bemused, *like a rabbit.*

"Built sometime in the 1900s, I guess. It's been vacant for a while. Renovations called for patience most people on the market didn't have, so post-foreclosure the bank auctioned it. I won, used it as a live-in project, started with the porch, then the kitchen, now I'm tiling the primary bathroom."

Colin hummed, glancing at the high ceiling and the faded, floral wallpaper. Still, the house refused to take a breath. "And the peculiarities?"

Bishop wrung their hands. Their slender throat worked around a swallow. "I started losing track of my tools after the first two weeks, I guess. Found a socket wrench in the freezer on a Tuesday morning. Nail gun in the dishwasher; gardening shears balanced upright on the blades. Noticed the drawers in an old dresser turned upside down. Things got progressively worse after that."

"Your email mentioned noises?" Colin traced the tall white baseboards—new, certainly—and the blue tape surrounding one, two, three archways in the hall.

Bishop walked and Colin followed, listening and cataloging as they spoke. "Voices, sometimes. *Disembodied* voices is the proper term, I guess. My name"—they pointed upward—"called from the second story. Pacing in the rooms upstairs when I'm downstairs; footsteps downstairs, usually in the kitchen, when I'm upstairs. I close more doors than I open," they said, and paused in front of a peeking closet, grasping the knob and pushing until it clicked shut. "It wasn't a big deal at first, you know. Livable."

"And what made it *un*livable?" Colin asked. He trailed Bishop into a spacious kitchen and set his briefcase on the floor beside a rustic barnwood picnic table.

The unmoored house leaned into silence. Colin did too. He tipped his head and pushed a gloved hand through his short auburn hair, attention pinned to Bishop's dusty brown boots shuffling toward the stove.

"Tea?" Bishop asked, sighing over the word. "Or coffee? I've got beer, but you don't look like an IPA before noon type of guy." They quirked their lips and tucked their thumbs through the belt loops on their blue jeans.

Colin lifted his brows. "I'll have whatever you're having."

Bishop's crooked smile broadened. "Beer it is."

The time—11:03 a.m.—glowed on the microwave, but Colin stayed quiet as Bishop reached into the fridge, coiled their fingers around two frosty beers, and snapped the caps off each bottleneck. They handed one to Colin and sipped from their own.

For eight years, Colin Hart had made oddities his line of work. Ghost wrangling, poltergeist politics, spirit deliverance, demonic ascension, vampiric theft, occult displacement, seaside anomalies—anything and everything "other" that accidentally or purposefully occupied a place it, technically, shouldn't. Most folks didn't have a use for him, but those who did, people like Bishop, never failed to reach out. And houses like this, houses with heartbeats, never failed to spark Colin's interest.

Interest aside, he wasn't partial to drinking in the morning. He sipped the skunky beer anyway and met Bishop's wide-set brown eyes. "Where were we, Bishop?"

"Livability," Bishop said, inhaling a long, drawn-out breath. They drained a third of their beer in one pull and leaned their hip against the marble countertop, all swirling silver and cobalt gray. They turned toward a sliding door and the fenced yard beyond the glass. "I've started hallucinating," they blurted, and closed their eyes, taking another deep breath. "I think I have, at least. I can't sleep, I'm seeing things I shouldn't, I caught myself having a conversation with . . . with nothing. Literally, *nothing*."

"Or something," Colin said matter-of-factly.

"Yeah, maybe." Bishop rested the bottle against their plush, pink mouth.

Colin course-corrected his thoughts—plush to poltergeist, pink to perpetual haunting—and sipped his beer too. "Would you mind if I took a look around? I know we talked about it over email, but I usually like to stay with clients if I choose to work on a space. Especially a home. Do you have a spare room available? I'll happily take the couch if—"

"No, no. The couch isn't, like, *bad*, but it's barely nap worthy. I've got a guest room ready. I'm happy to give you a tour if you'd like,"

Bishop said, jutting their chin toward a cracked door across from the dining area. "Unless you need to, I don't know, *explore*."

"Please," Colin said, extending his arm. "Lead the way."

Bishop drank as they walked, tipping their buzzed head back to drain the rest of their beer. Colin plucked at his beige turtleneck and slid a compact leather notebook from the inside pocket of his coat.

"I can hang that for you," Bishop said.

Colin tucked a ballpoint pen behind his ear and traded the bottle from one hand to the other as he shrugged away his coat, folding it neatly before holding the garment out to Bishop. "That'd be lovely, actually."

Bishop knitted their brows. They echoed the word soundlessly, allowing their mouth to make the shape—*lovely*—and hung Colin's coat in the hall closet.

"We'll start with the basement, yeah?" They tilted their head and took long strides across the room, toeing open a fissured door. An exposed bulb hummed above the wooden staircase, disappearing into thick shadow. "Washer and dryer are down here, but other than that it's just storage space. Nothin' special."

"Any activity?" Colin listened to their shoes bounce on the creaky stairs.

Another bulb flashed. Ugly yellow light washed across bare concrete, illuminating stainless steel shelves stocked with linens, the washer and dryer against the far wall, cardboard boxes taped shut, and a recliner, rocking gently, occupied by something and nothing.

An eyeless face stretched into a snout. Pale hands perched on the armrests. Tailored suit, black on black, hugged lean muscle. Wolf head, human body.

There and gone, as if the click of the switch had chased the creature away. It disappeared in a blink. Hot saliva pooled in Colin's mouth.

He swallowed, scanning the room for another ghost, demon, ghoul. Anything. But whoever, *whatever*, had given him that beastly attention had slipped away. Nothing except a famished chair remained.

"It's a basement, so . . ." Bishop shrugged, unfazed by the apparition. "Kinda creepy as-is."

"You've never felt anything?"

"Watched."

The sheer blonde hair on Colin's arms prickled beneath his cashmere sweater. "Noted. Next?"

He kept his eyes on the stairs as they climbed and sipped from the half-full bottle pinched between his knuckles. Bishop guided him through the living room, modestly decorated with inlaid bookshelves and a buttery leather sofa. The coffee table was adorned with a succulent terrarium, and a flat-screen hung above a yawning mantel, home to charred logs and ashen brick. It was right then, right there, when the house decided to breathe. Colin heard the soft, gushing sound of lived-in beams and thin walls expanding like a lung. Eaves suckled at the ceiling and doors rattled gently on their hinges. Colin felt the presence of something large, comfortable, and certain press inward through the house's skeleton, studying the two of them with vague interest.

"See?" Bishop said. They jabbed their finger at the hall closet. The door floated open, just barely.

Colin ran his tongue across his bottom lip. "Noted," he said again, and gestured toward the staircase. "Shall we?"

Bishop skipped their ruddy hand along the banister. Colin steered his eyes from the crisscrossed veins on their wrist to the place an apparition had stooped upon his arrival. Only an imprint remained, as if a freezer had opened and closed on the second-to-last step, blowing icy air around his ankles. A standing fan spun in an empty, doorless room, and tools littered stained carpet outside the primary bedroom at the end of the hall.

"I hear pacing at night. Sometimes walking, sometimes running, or . . . or crawling, I guess. The window in that room never stays closed," Bishop said, and jutted their thumb at the unfinished bedroom. They opened the door across from it, furnished with a honey oak bed set and simple white bedding. "You'd stay here if you decide to investigate. The guest bathroom is completely renovated—new showerhead, tile, vanity, and toilet."

"Is there an attic?" Colin asked.

"Yeah, but it's empty. No one built it out."

"And your hallucinations?" He walked through the double doors and surveyed Bishop's bedroom. Chic bamboo blinds, puffy comforter, wicker laundry hamper, macramé wall decor. In the attached bathroom, the vanity was dismantled, claw-foot tub gleaming, mirror cracked in the center.

"They're hard to explain." Bishop averted their eyes to the ground. Their face darkened and they cleared their throat, nudging their chin toward the hall. "Have you seen what you need to in here?"

"Yes, actually." Colin noticed the Juliet balcony as he spun on his heels, hurrying from the room. "I have a travel bag with me. Are there any guidelines I should follow during my stay? Work hours I should know about? Dietary allergies? Partners, roommates?"

He glided his palm across the banister the same way Bishop had and paused before the front door, searching for another apparition, listening for a whisper. The only thing he came away with was Bishop's caught breath and their steady gaze.

Their lips parted, surprised. "You'll do it then? The . . . the cleaning? You'll—"

"Do my best. You saw my website. I can't offer guarantees, but yes, I will attempt to clean your home if you'd like to hire me. You've reviewed my rates?"

"I have, yeah."

"Excellent."

"And no to the guidelines, I guess. Do your dishes, obviously. No allergies, no partner, no roommate. It's just me."

"It isn't," Colin said, studying the foyer again.

"Excuse me?"

"Just you," he rasped, and cleared his throat. "I'll get my things. You can wire me the deposit anytime within the next twenty-four hours."

Bishop blinked, taken aback. "Oh," they chirped, mouth squirming. "Right, yeah. I'll do that."

Colin Hart opened the front door. He felt heavy for a moment. Watched. Uninvited. On his way back from the car with his compact, rolling suitcase, he spotted a face in the reflection on the porch window—snarling muzzle, vivid eyes, pointed ears—and Bishop Martínez, blurred and pensive, seated on the couch beyond it.

CHAPTER TWO

C OLIN LEFT THE BEDROOM DOOR ajar as he unpacked. He
tucked folded shirts into the empty dresser and draped tailored corduroy pants, pressed denim, and neat trousers over individual
hangers next to high-necked sweaters and button-down shirts. The
first few nights in a new home were always a bit awkward—*obviously*—but he usually found himself overwhelmed by his hosts. Suffocated, really. *Anything we can do? Can we help? Fix you somethin', maybe?
Coffee? Tea?* Always wringing hands; always war-torn and worried.
Helicopter homeowners hoping for a miracle.

Thankfully, Bishop kept to their bedroom, fiddling with tile and
cement. Loud whacks came and went. Curses, whimpers, heavy sighs.
Afterward, the pipes groaned and howled, the shower ran, and Colin
took his chance to wander the house on his own. He lingered on the
stairs, shuffling his wool socks along each step, and felt for the emp-
ty-eyed ghost he'd spotted there before. The environment felt tainted.
Tense, almost. Like something rancid had been overturned and left
to fester. Even so, he noticed vanilla wafting from downstairs, spread
by a candle aptly titled *Grandma's Cookies*. Colin brushed his covered
thumb along the back of the couch, watching a divot cut through the

fluffy throw blanket, and tipped his head toward the archway leading into the adjoining dining room.

Crowded houses rarely made themselves known to strangers. They waited, courting their regular occupiers with budding tension and tested boundaries. Colin hadn't earned his place yet, but he typically didn't have to: haunted places never failed to recognize haunted people.

"C'mon," he mumbled, taking brisk steps into the kitchen.

No voice greeted him. No wolf-headed being appeared. No sound cut the quiet until the stairs coughed beneath quick, light steps. Colin pretended to admire the floating shelves, stocked with coffee mugs, decorative dishes, crystal glassware, and squirrel-shaped salt and pepper shakers. Copper pots hung from hooks stamped into fresh navy paint and a cast-iron skillet sat on the stove, purposefully placed, waiting for a forgotten meal.

"Oh—*Jesus*. Hi," Bishop said, catching their breath. "You . . . damn, you scared me."

Colin turned. His eyes clipped damp collarbones. He snapped his gaze to Bishop's face, apple red from a scalding shower.

"Apologies." He cleared awkwardness from his throat. "You didn't answer me before. Your hallucinations," he prompted, tripping delicately over each syllable. "I understand your reluctance, but it *is* required information . . ." His lips pressed, halfway to *mx*. "Bishop," he concluded.

Bishop scrubbed their palm over their buzzed hair, gaze drifting toward the ceiling. "I hear you. We'll talk about it over dinner, yeah? I need to run out for some sealant. This bathroom is a bitch to get right, but I'm hoping to finish it by tomorrow night."

"Sure, that's fine," Colin said.

"Usually I cook, but there's a really good Indian place next to the hardware shop. Fan of curry?"

"Chicken korma, please. Extra rice."

Bishop's brows slouched. A smile sprang to their face, unprompted. "Straight to the point, huh?"

Colin blushed terribly. He clasped his gloved hands. "It's appreciated in my field."

"So I've gathered. How 'bout tea?"

"Yes, I like tea."

"With milk?"

"Yes—yeah, milk is fine."

Bishop nodded, assessing Colin with an inquisitive once-over. "Got it," they said, laughing in their throat. "Anything else?"

"No, that'll do. I have cash, I can—"

"My treat," they said. "You good alone?"

Colin smiled briefly. "Yeah, I'll set up the surveillance gear while you're gone."

"Right, yeah. Forgot about that. Well, feel free to raid the fridge. There isn't much, but . . ." They shrugged, twirling their key chain around their finger. "I'll be back tonight."

Bishop paused in the hallway and opened the closet, shrugging their arms into a well-worn flannel jacket with a sheepskin collar. After that, they walked through the front door, an engine stubbornly turned over in the driveway, and they were gone.

The house changed in their absence—inhaled and exhaled, rattled and shook.

"Oh, stop that," Colin rasped, glancing from the swaying chandelier above the table to the locked slider straining to open. "If you don't plan on showing yourself, then behave at least."

Everything quieted. Spiraled like a tired child after a tantrum. He held his hand open, palm parallel to the ceiling, and waited for cool fingertips to grace his skin, breath to encase his knuckles, teeth to latch around his wrist. He frowned and heaved an irritated sigh. Whatever nested in the rafters and flowed freely through the floorboards refused to touch him.

He tried again, flexing his fingers inward, closing his eyes, centering his energy, and reached for presence, for magic, for displacement.

There, he thought. *Yes, there you are.*

When Colin opened his eyes, his breath hitched, and he found himself confronted. Knifelike bone pressed hard against thin skin, bending the creature's flesh like a curtain over rod iron. The apparition he'd seen on the staircase stood before him, lips sawed away, pulled back to expose receding gums and square teeth. Its eyes were pits, caving inward toward pale muscle and bloodless tissue. Hair stringed in mangled patches from its skull, and its knobby, girlish fingers hovered like a marionette above his hand.

I see.

"Man of God," the spirit croaked, "do you find me wanting?"

Colin lifted his free hand and made the sign of the cross in front of its forehead.

"I find you damned," he whispered.

When the creature touched Colin's palm, he seized its icy fingers and squeezed, wrenching it through the shared space where *there* met *elsewhere*. He curled his hand around its narrow throat. His knuckles buckled inward, cutting away a long-spent life. Things like this never ended quickly—unfinished things, angry things. But Colin had the touch, the sense, the profound ability to communicate with restless, vengeful horrors. For twenty-seven years he'd communicated with the dead. For five years he'd called it a business. For six years he'd tried to earn his way back into God's good graces.

If God existed, of course.

"Prince of the Heavenly Host, I ask you to guide this child," Colin said. In his grasp, the creature howled. "Michael, protector, Saint in the Armory, deliver this soul as you see fit. Take this ruin and make it new."

The creature belched smoke, screeching and writhing, reaching for the ceiling, for an impossibly bright light that poured through the windows. Ink burned, etched into the milky skin beneath Colin's sweater, and he watched the ghoul disintegrate. The release always hurt. Sending a spirit into the arms of next—whatever *next* may be—felt like clipping a bone with a scalpel.

He winced as the creature jerked and spasmed, peeling away into a cloud of rapidly dissolving ash. Once it was gone and its strangled death-cries faded, Colin swayed on his feet, listening to the house hold its breath.

"Aim your grievances at me," he said, clearing his chalky throat. "I'm here to cut you away from this place—somewhere you're not meant to be. Force my hand, and it will hurt. Go willingly, and I'll extract you as gently as possible. But the homeowner is not the exorcist in this equation. Truthfully, I wouldn't call myself that either." He let his shoulders go heavy and sighed at the tense ceiling. Something, a few things, turned their eyes on him, watching from their hidden spots in the hollow walls and rusted keyholes. "But it is what it is, and I am what I am."

Colin rarely opened a case with a violent departure, but he needed this house to understand. He needed the beings who had crammed themselves into the wood and tile and cement and shingles to see what he could do. And now that they'd witnessed him, he needed to capture them.

As his muscles slowly unwound, he went to work arranging cameras in the corner of each room. Tested battery life, line-of-sight, movement detection, night vision, and temperature gauges. Made notes about gear placement and sketched a rough depiction of the creature he'd released. Probably a ghoulish watermark from a long-ago life, perhaps a vindictive ghost looking for revenge. Either way, he'd felt its unwillingness to leave and wondered about the rest of the obscure things caged in the house.

Excavation might prove to be difficult, he thought. *What's keeping them here?*

Once the cameras were live, Colin tested their connection to his laptop, sitting propped open and humming on the coffee table. He hadn't noticed the sun sinking low, sending shards of pink and orange across the sky, until Bishop opened the front door, and a pastel kaleidoscope haloed their shoulders. Hours had come and gone, eaten by Colin's overanalytical tendencies—fixing this, installing that, feeling for energetic spikes, and listening to the house splinter through an exhale. Time had been stolen, somehow. Altered. He blinked, taken aback, and cleared his throat.

"I've fixed the cameras. Two in the living room, one in the kitchen, two others—one wide-angle, one zoom—on the staircase, one in the hallway, each guest room, and your bedroom," Colin said. He pointed to the closed door across the room. "And the basement, of course. There's all-weather equipment in the backyard, angled toward the slider."

Bishop pawed through a plastic bag, setting white take-out boxes on the counter one by one.

"My bedroom," they said, raspy and unsure. "That's necessary?"

"Typically, yes. I can remove them if you'd like, but I assume you've experienced peculiarities there as well?"

"Peculiarities," they muttered, nodding as they plated rice, curry, and charred naan. They shot him a curious look. "Are you always this formal . . . ? Because you can say *ghost* or *haunting* or . . . or, fuck, I don't know, *poltergeist*."

"Would you prefer—"

"Oh my *God*."

"This *does* happen to be my business, Bishop. Forgive me for being polite," he snapped. Heat rushed into his face, surely blotching his fair complexion. He'd never been badgered by a client before. Not about formality, at least.

Bishop set his plate on the table next to his laptop along with his tea, snapped the cap off a cold beer, and set that down as well. They tipped their head, smiling slyly.

"Forgive me for being *fucking* polite." Colin rested the bottle against his mouth. "Better?"

"Much," Bishop said, and swung their legs over the bench seat across from him. "Can I ask how you got into . . . this?"

"It's not a complicated story. I heard the dead, I saw the dead, I began to communicate with the dead. Things spiraled from there. Once I realized I wasn't speaking exclusively with ghosts, I started researching the occult, and, well . . ." He shrugged, forking rice into his mouth. That wasn't the whole truth, but it was true enough. "Here I am."

"Here you are," Bishop said matter-of-factly. "You look young. I mean, I assumed you were young, but you make it sound like you've been at this for—"

"I'm twenty-seven," Colin said, frowning. "Do I *look* older . . . ?"

"No, but you *sound* older."

"You're, what, twenty-three?"

"Twenty-*five*." Bishop snorted.

"Okay, twenty-five." Colin pushed his sleeves to his elbows. Bishop's eyes flicked, tracking the black sigils inked into his skin. Crisp edges, swirling curves—ancient angelic language—diving from his wrist to the crook of his elbow. He ignored their prying—*rude*—and dunked naan into reddish-orange curry puddled next to his rice. "Tell me about these hallucinations."

They lowered their gaze to their plate. "Is that proper dinner conversation?"

"It is tonight."

"Yeah, okay," they said, pushing rice around with their fork. They nodded and clucked their tongue, inhaled deeply, exhaling sharply. "I caught myself having conversations with my reflection while I was working in the guest bathroom. It's like I was talking to myself, but not. I've been alone in this house for six months, so talking out loud just . . . just happened, you know? But then I realized I was answering questions. Like, questions spoken from somewhere else. Below me, behind me. At one point, I didn't recognize my reflection. I'd open my mouth and my reflection wouldn't. I'd take a step; my reflection would stay put. I . . ." They tapped their fork against their plate. "I started sleepwalking. Following someone—some*thing*. I woke up in the basement, once. On the floor next to my bed. Then outside."

"Outside?"

"On the porch, yeah. Against the front door."

"Do you remember what you were being asked?"

Bishop paused to chew. "No," they said, too quietly. "No, I don't remember anything. I'd finish whatever I was doing and try to recall *why* I was talking. I never could."

Colin nodded. *Strange.* He offered a smile. *They're lying.* "When's the last time this happened?"

"Three days ago. That's when I woke up outside."

"And have you noticed any defining characteristics in any of the apparitions around the house?"

"The only one I've ever seen is the crone. She's—"

"Taken care of," Colin said, draining the rest of his beer. "Quite skeletal, right? Hairless, eyeless, gaping mouth?"

Bishop drummed on their amber bottle. Their eyes narrowed, lips parting for a slow, mindful breath.

"Yes," they said, and reached out to tap one of Colin's tattoos, centered over the top of his wrist. "What're these?"

Most people stared, but never asked. He glanced at Bishop's fingers, spiderlike, tickling his skin. Turning his arm over, he rested the back of his hand flat against the table. Bishop continued to touch him, tracing the hard-edged marks scrawled across his freckled limb.

"Protection," he said, and drew his hand away, balancing his fingertip on the pale tan line at the base of Bishop's ring finger. "What's this?"

They tucked their hand into their lap. "Protection," they parroted, and went back to eating.

Strange, Colin thought, watching them. *That sounded like the truth.*

Chapter Three

THE FIRST NIGHT, COLIN WOKE to footsteps pitter-pattering in the hallway. He stared at the ceiling, propped on a freshly washed pillow, awake in the shadowy guest bedroom. Tracked them, one by one, back and forth, as they crossed the doorway. He waited, listening to the floor creak and a patch of light bend around the door. Like a flashlight, maybe.

In his nightshirt and joggers, he slipped out of bed and took careful steps toward the door. He gripped the knob and pushed.

Bishop trudged from their open bedroom past the guest bathroom, and walked in front of Colin. Their eyes were unblinking, fixed on something in the distance. Empty, but open. They walked with purpose—asleep but not, awake but gone—and stopped on the landing at the top of the staircase. The house breathed easily. Inhaling and exhaling, bending toward them and yawning open, struck silently alive in the early hours after midnight. Bishop swayed. Turned. Stared back toward their bedroom and then, slowly, began to reach.

The wolf-headed creature manifested like mist. Came forth in front of Bishop, dressed in a fine tailored suit, and rested human hands on each side of their neck. They held each other carefully, the same way lovers would.

"I'm sorry," Bishop said.

Colin leaned around the doorframe. The floor wheezed and his heart plummeted into his stomach. *Damn*.

The wolf-man whipped around, snarling. But as Bishop buckled forward, looking to be caught, the apparition disintegrated, and Bishop fell to their knees in the middle of the hall. Colin glanced at the camera hooked to the ceiling and hoped it managed to catch what he'd just seen.

He crept toward Bishop, crouching in front of them.

"Bishop," Colin said, softly at first, then louder, "Bishop, hey. Are you awake?"

They blinked, shoulders slumping, expression gentling. "What're you doin'?"

"You were sleepwalking. We're in the hall."

They swiped at their eyes and glanced at the wetness on the back of their hand.

"Oh," they said, surprised, and sniffled. "Did I say anything?"

"You said you were sorry."

At that, Bishop's chin dimpled. "Oh . . . well, I . . . I *am* sorry for waking you," they blurted, then stumbled to their feet, walking briskly into their bedroom. The door shut with a click.

Colin waited there, kneeling on the floor, staring at the place Bishop and the wolf-man had stood. The air thickened, as if the house turned inside out, displaying its vulnerabilities to the night. To Colin. Especially to Bishop. Something had happened there—something terrible and heart wrenching. Something Bishop hadn't shared. Something brutally personal.

Colin glanced down the staircase and stared into the opaque darkness. He didn't know what or who, but something stared back at him. Something who knew this place, and knew Bishop, and knew the whole damn story.

"Do you have anything to say?" Colin whispered.

Gently, like a butterfly, two words landed on the shell of his ear.

"*Get out.*"

Colin woke to the smell of bacon grease and buttermilk batter. He stood at the window, watching dew glint on naked branches, and recalled how the wolf-headed apparition held Bishop, tenderly and lovingly, in the hallway the night before. He glanced at his laptop, seated on the nightstand with his journal, then turned his eyes toward the camera in the corner.

What happened here? He leaned closer to the window, watching a fat finch flutter in the driveway. His breath fanned, fogging the glass, revealing streaks from a fingertip. He blew gently. Messy words appeared—*I do I do I do*—above a thumbprint heart. He fumbled for his phone. Snapped a picture and watched each word fade. *What did you two do to each other?*

The staircase wheezed. Knuckles rapped his bedroom door, knocking it ajar. Colin turned, met with Bishop dressed in a slouchy, striped long-sleeve—cliff-edged collarbones and long throat and slender shoulders—leaning on the doorframe.

"Hope you like pancakes," they said, and wrung their hands. "Anything else happen last night?"

Colin almost pointed to the window. Almost said *yes.* "No. Quiet as a church."

Bishop nodded, but they seemed altogether unconvinced. "And the footage . . . ?"

"I haven't given it a look yet. I can bring my laptop downstairs, though, if you'd like to do an overview with me."

"Yeah, I'd, uh, I'd like to see what you saw, if that makes sense."

"It does," Colin said. He swallowed, paying mind to his own body, something he rarely put on display. Thin pink scars beneath his nipples, exposed ink on his bare chest—black sigils and thorny vines, angelic runes, and biblical script. Bishop's eyes jolted from the low line of his joggers to the inverted cross tattooed in the soft hollow at the base of his throat.

Bishop met his eyes and blinked, suddenly caught. They turned swiftly toward the hall. "I'll cut some fruit," they said over their shoulder.

"Be right there," Colin said.

They're beautiful. The thought intruded. Honest, but unnecessary. Abrupt and complicated and completely unprofessional. He heaved a sigh, forcing his mind to quiet.

He dressed in black pencil pants, plaid socks, and a brown knitted sweater, and stopped by the guest bathroom to brush his teeth and rake texturizer through his short hair. Unsurprisingly, the house had already printed dark circles beneath his eyes, a sign of sleeplessness he couldn't shake away. He stared at his black pupils. Scrubbed deodorant under his arms and tipped his head, pressing two fingers to his reshaped jaw, dragging the digits over his slender throat, halting at the place an Adam's apple should've been.

For years, Colin Hart had searched for oddities and spirits, ripped unwelcome breath from between the bones of crowded houses, braced for fangs and claws in demonic dwellings, but he'd never managed to scrape the inconsistencies out of himself. Hips, too wide. Shoulders, too narrow. Wrists, too small. Testosterone be damned, he still felt half-framed and hollow. As if his body was a home with too many unused rooms, too much open space. A place still under construction.

Focus, he thought. Splashing his face and dabbing his skin dry with a towel, vision blurred by his damp eyelashes, Colin noticed something unfurl in the mirror. Glowing, almost. As if a shard of sunlight had cracked through the glass. It blinked. Spread. Became almond shaped and alive. An eye, assessing him with quick, mindful flicks. Gold and bronze surrounded by black and pitted with an onyx pupil.

"Hello," Colin whispered.

The same two words from last night sparked in the bathroom. "*Get out*," growled and snapped, accompanied by the click of teeth. That suspended eye crinkled angrily, canine and furious, before it disappeared, abandoning Colin's reflection.

"You comin'?" Bishop hollered. Plates clinked and grease popped.

Colin left the bathroom, grabbed his laptop, and pressed his feet firmly against each stair, searing what he'd witnessed into his memory. The house strained, crumbling inward to watch him—to make him *feel* watched. Beams and walls and foundation followed his long strides through the hall like a cat following a fly.

He stepped into the kitchen, sweetly scented and stove-warmed, and ignored the many gazes peering at him from hidden places.

"The wolf," Colin said immediately. He watched Bishop pause, go rigid, lock up. "Have you seen it?"

"*Him*," Bishop corrected. They cleared their throat and angled a spatula, sliding fluffy pancakes onto a plate. "He has masculine vibes, don't you think?"

"So you've seen him."

"Couple times."

"Bishop."

"Colin." They sighed his name, then shot him a tight glance. "Low-sugar maple syrup or blackberry jam?"

"You've hired me to clean your house, but I can't properly assess the situation if issues are being kept from me."

Bishop clenched their jaw, finally relenting. "The weird wolf-man has appeared a few times. Once on the staircase, once in my bedroom, once in a reflection on the window while I was cleaning—"

"Last night in the hallway," Colin added, matter-of-factly. He took the plate fixed with cakes, crispy bacon, orange slices, and juicy green grapes.

"I thought it was a dream. I didn't . . . The wolf-man wasn't who I *saw*."

"And who did you see?"

"Doesn't matter," Bishop said. They sat at the table and cut into their pancakes, stuffing their mouth with sticky pastry. "You've got the footage. That'll probably help you a lot more than whatever I dream about."

"You'd be surprised. Dreams are uniquely informative." Colin sat across from them. He glanced at his dry pancakes and cocked his head. "Is there . . . ?"

Bishop pushed the syrup toward him. "You never answered me," they quipped.

He narrowed his eyes, took the bottle, and poured a generous amount over his cakes. He dragged a piece of bacon through puddled syrup and brought it to his mouth. "Where were we? Right, dreams. You'd rather not share, I'm guessing?"

"Yeah, we'll skip that." Bishop's fine features twisted into an unpleasant frown. "Footage," they prompted, gesturing to Colin's laptop. "Can I see?"

Colin lifted an eyebrow. "Eager."

"You would be too."

He opened his laptop and clicked on the archived recordings from the previous twelve hours, setting the speed to triple, then fast-forwarding until Bishop left their bedroom and walked into the hall. Colin slowed the video and turned the laptop, watching the tension drain from Bishop's expression, replaced by something close to sadness.

They stared at their captured image. Stepping into the hallway. Reaching into the darkness.

No wolf-man stood with them. No ghost appeared. But Bishop reacted to a touch, a presence. Their body language melted into pliant familiarity, and their voice came through the speakers, weak and timid. *I'm sorry.* The video played through Colin's interruption and Bishop's awkward shuffle back to their bedroom. Colin stopped the recording.

"Unfortunately, the apparition didn't translate on video," Colin said. "But you certainly saw something. I did too."

"Certainly." Their breath quivered, but they shielded apprehension, pain, grief, whatever they'd refused to share, and faced their breakfast. "Do you have any ideas?"

"About your house? Standard ideas, yes. Nothing concrete."

Bishop met his eyes, waiting expectantly.

"Honestly, I think whatever we're dealing with is attached to you, not the house. It's sentient, obviously. Protective, maybe. I wouldn't say nefarious if I didn't already know it'd driven you outside in the middle of winter." He paused, rolling the next word around in his mouth before adding, "Jealous. Envious of you, I think. Whatever it is, it's powerful enough to evade being recorded, and brave enough to show itself to me."

"*Brave*," Bishop mimicked, chuckling under their breath. "That's an interesting word."

"Is it?"

"It is," they said. "Do you have a plan?"

"I wish I did, but no, not yet. I need a little more time. I hope being here isn't a distraction—"

"It's not. You're welcome to stay as long as you need to."

"Good," Colin said. Something hot and new twinged in his chest. *It's this house*, he thought. *Clinging to every sip of heat.*

A beat of silence surfaced, broken by forks on plates and teeth tugging at food. Bishop stared at the table. Silvered sunlight beamed through the cloud cover and passed through the slider, glowing on their bronze skin. They shifted their eyes, settling their gaze on Colin's face.

"How long ago did you transition?" they asked, then wrinkled their nose, opening and closing their mouth. "I'm sorry, I didn't mean to . . . Fuck, I mean, *I did*, but—"

"Technically, twelve years ago," Colin said. He shrugged, running his bottom lip along the rim of his glass. He swallowed pulpy grapefruit juice. "But I started medically transitioning when I was eighteen. You?"

"Three years. Still new."

"You're pretty young to be a homeowner. Did you get this place by yourself or . . . ?"

Bishop bit into an orange slice. "No, I didn't. But it's mine now. That's what matters."

"Did anyone else ever live here? Not to be invasive, but if you'd like me to do my job then I need to know."

"Yeah, briefly," Bishop said. They crunched a grape, drank their juice, and breathed slowly, deeply. "But like I said, it's mine now."

Colin hummed. He knew better than to press. Clocked Bishop's shielded eyes, their tense shoulders, and ate the rest of his food.

"Thank you for breakfast."

"Don't worry about it. I like to cook." Bishop attempted to take Colin's plate, but he stopped them.

"Let me," he said, and took both of their plates to the sink, soaping the imitation porcelain with a sponge under lukewarm water. "Any plans for today?"

"Installing the new shower doors."

"Then your bedroom is done?"

"Yeah, finally. I might run to the nursery for some plants. Give this place a little life."

"Want company? I'd like to leave the house for a while. Test its tolerance for loneliness."

Bishop nodded curtly. "Sure, yeah. You can help me pick out some greenery," they said, striding through the foyer. "We'll leave around noon."

"Okay," Colin said. He leaned against the counter, watching the glass slider catch Bishop's transparent reflection. They walked through the hall, paused at the staircase, and Colin saw the ghostly whisper of hands on their waist, slipping across them, holding on to them, causing their lips to pop open and their eyes to close.

What did you two do to each other? Colin thought, watching Bishop's splotchy reflection sway, blur, bend. He turned away once footsteps hit the stairs. *What did you two mean to each other?*

CHAPTER FOUR

M OON STRIKE NURSERY LIVED ON the outskirts of Gideon, Colorado, a mere fifteen minutes away from the house on Staghorn Way. Colin followed Bishop through the cluttered metaphysical shop crowded with tarot cards, jewelry, gardening tools, and crystal specimens, and walked into the attached greenhouse. Flat brown pots lined the dewy walls, and shelves stacked with sprouts and propagation vials filled the room. Houseplants sat atop long tables next to flower-bed starters and assorted herbs. He touched an eye-shaped leaf the size of his hand and framed an orchid bulb between his knuckles.

"This place is quite *witchy*," Colin said, smiling around the last word.

Bishop turned a terra-cotta pot from side to side, studying a prickly cactus. "Best prices in town," they said, setting the pot down, picking up another. "Nothin' wrong with a little magic, right?"

"Depends on the magic."

They set the cactus down and rounded the table, standing across from Colin. A green vine rested in the crook of their thumb.

The side of Bishop's mouth lifted. "So what makes a house lonely?"

Colin peeled his eyes away from Bishop's slender hand and focused on their face, flushed from the warm climate brewing in the greenhouse. He considered his answer. Abandonment. Unfinished business. There was always something or some*one* that caused a house to want, to ache, to make itself known. There was always a reason for anger and lust and becoming lonesome.

"It depends on the circumstances. If the entity imprints on its death marker or on a memory from inside the house, then usually the home is fairly easy to clean. If the entity is attached to a person, it becomes more difficult. Almost like an exorcism of the heart, so to speak."

"The heart but not the body?" Bishop braved, striding slowly along the table. Flowers bent beneath their palm. Greenery shifted under their wrists and forearms as they reached for baby monsteras and unfurled roses.

"Depends. If the entity imprinted on the heart, then I focus on the heart. If something imprinted on the body . . ." He tipped his head, considering. "Then I exorcise the body."

"And if it's both?"

"It usually isn't."

"But if it is?" Bishop lifted their eyes.

Heat coiled beneath Colin's navel, striking in his groin. His throat flexed around a swallow. "Then I exorcise the body *and* the heart. Separately, sometimes. At once, if necessary."

"And what's that like?"

"Why?" Colin asked, turning his attention to a lanky philodendron. "Are you afraid I'll have to exorcise you, Bishop? Is that what we're getting at?"

"I'm not afraid of anything," Bishop said. They grabbed the plant Colin had been studying. Vines tapped their waist as they hauled an armful of ferns and foliage toward the register, pausing to jut their chin at a row of clay pots. "Can you grab three of those? Two medium, one large."

Colin collected the pots and set them on the cash-wrap inside Moon Strike's metaphysical shop. Hand-carved spirit boards were propped on velvet stands behind the counter, and crystal wind chimes caught the muted sunlight, spinning slowly from the ceiling. The woman behind the register regarded Bishop with practiced familiarity, darting her eyes at Colin while she wrapped their terra-cotta and placed their plants in a cardboard carrier.

The woman adjusted her name tag—Tehlor—and cleared her throat. "How're those prayer beads treatin' you, Bishop? Still keepin' bad spirits at bay?"

"The prayer beads are for meditation, but the cleansing bundle did wonders. Thank you," Bishop said, handing over their debit card.

"Is that why you hired a cleaner?"

Colin stilled. Every muscle went rigid beneath his skin. He glanced at the rosy ink clustered on her throat, tracked the chlorine-blonde braid flopped over her shoulder, and met her clever, upturned eyes. "And what would a witch know about a cleaner?"

"Enough," Tehlor said, and slid Bishop's card across the cash-wrap.

"Colin comes highly recommended. And . . . I don't know. Sometimes a mess is too dirty to handle yourself," Bishop said.

Colin hummed. "Or too personal."

Tehlor's lips hinted at a smile. "Or too personal," she echoed, and tucked a folded receipt into the box with Bishop's plants. "If you need another cleansing bundle, you know where I am."

Bishop glanced between Colin and Tehlor. They furrowed their brow playfully. "Okay, Miss *Witch*. I'll be sure to find you."

The shopkeeper propped her elbow on the counter, cradling her chin. "Don't know if you have the Keys in your collection, but I've got copies on standby. Might help."

"Keys?" Colin asked.

"Of Solomon," Bishop interjected. They tipped their head politely. "I'll leave the cleaning to Colin. See you around."

She offered a two-finger wave. "See you."

Colin noticed the sharply carved crystal strung around her neck on a glinting silver chain. Black tourmaline, maybe. Shaped like a hammer. He watched her index finger guide the stone back and forth, then turned and followed Bishop into the gravel parking lot.

Puffy dark clouds splotched the sky, shadowing Gideon, masking the white peaks on the horizon. *Keys.* He wasn't necessarily surprised, but the comfortability in Bishop's mouth when they uttered *of Solomon* and the familiarity between them and the local witch's den gave him pause. He hoisted into the passenger seat of Bishop's truck, scanning their stoic face.

"So do you know the Greater Key of Solomon or the Lesser—"

"Both," Bishop said, shrugging. "Not well, but enough. Why?"

"I wouldn't call them *light* reading."

"I took an astrology class a year ago. Learned about star guides and natal charts. Figured out why I have terrible taste in men," they teased, snorting. "Being a Gemini *rising* is the culprit, I guess. Go figure. Anyway, I bought the combined paperback after the Zoom conference. It was one of the host bookstore's 'recommended reads' for anyone interested in neo-pagan bullshit." They flashed a sarcastic grin and leveled a narrow-eyed look at Colin over the edge of their sunglasses. "Why? You worried I'm in bed with Mister Crowley? Think I'm sleazing around with a famous occultist?"

"I don't know who you crawl into bed with," Colin said, and put his sunglasses on, tipping his head against the seat to peer at Bishop's strong nose and pretty teeth, their sweeping eyelashes and lying smile. "But I get the feeling *knowing* might help me clean your house."

Bishop turned the key in the ignition. A thumb-sized mirror dangled from their key chain, sending muted sunlight bouncing around the truck cab. "Don't worry, Colin. I'm not fucking any magicians."

"You just know the local witch and live in a haunted house?"

"Is that what we're dealing with? A haunting? I like that much better than *peculiarity*."

"I wish I could confidently say *yes*, but I don't know. I have a feeling what's happening in your house, to you, around you, has reverberated from a secret." He met Bishop's eyes, then turned toward the window. "And I can't help you *or* your house until I know what you're hiding."

Laughter bloomed in their throat. They yanked the truck into drive and hit the gas. "Ask away, exorcist."

"You're a little young to be retired," Colin said.

"That's not a question."

"What do you do for work?"

"No one's too young to be retired military. Especially when retirement is polite lingo for honorable discharge which is even *worse* lingo for traumatic injury and PTSD. So nothin' right now. Working on the house, taking weird Zoom classes, being a stay-at-home plant parent."

They sighed, flicking the blinker, and Colin knew they were lying. Again.

"Injury, huh?"

"Training exercise. Broke two ribs, punctured a lung. Psych deemed me *unfit* for duty."

"Sorry," Colin said.

"Don't be."

"Who'd you apologize to last night?"

Bishop's breath halted. "I was dreaming—"

"About?"

"I don't know, honestly."

"*Honestly?*"

Bishop stomped the brake pedal at a red light. "I hired you to dig into my house, not to interrogate my goddamn personal life."

"So it *is* personal," he said, breath gusting from him on an exhausted sigh. "Mind telling me *how* personal?"

"I was dreaming about my husband," they snapped.

Silence snaked through the truck cab, broken by tires rolling across concrete, brakes squeaking in the driveway, Bishop shoving the gearshift into park. They gnawed their lip, facing forward in the driver's seat. Their thumbs crossed at the bottom of the steering wheel.

"My ex-husband," they clarified quietly. "That's all."

Colin swallowed. Heat filled his cheeks, but he tipped his chin and remembered the words written in steam on the guest bedroom window. *I do I do I do.* How tenderly the wolf-headed creature held them, how gently and fully they'd fallen into its arms.

He inhaled a long, deep breath. "You said you didn't have a partner."

Bishop snared him in an angry glare. "Because I don't," they said, then grabbed the box from the back seat and slammed the driver's side door, rattling the rearview mirror.

The passenger visor came loose. Colin startled, sighing through his nose as a Polaroid fluttered onto his lap. He pinched it by the white corner and studied the faded image. Bishop, laughing. Eyes creased, shoulders loose, head tipped to accommodate another mouth. Lidded eyes stared back at them, paired with a soft smile, and fingers curled beneath their chin. Knuckle ringed in gold. Lips close.

Colin flipped the photo over, tracing words written in cursive with his fingertip: *Our night. Rehearsal dinner.*

Colin stopped in the entryway and listened to the door swing shut at his back.

Fear sometimes happened all at once—seeping into his skeleton, rushing fast in his veins—and sometimes it happened slowly. A spear sinking through the soles of his feet, sliding behind his kneecaps, burrowing into his stomach. That slow fear radiated through him, thickening as he glanced from the camera balancing on the base of the banister to the lenses plucked from their stands in the living room and perched on the couch. Recording devices ripped from the walls and arranged in a pyramid in the center of the hallway. Bishop stood in the archway leading to the kitchen, arms folded across their chest, turned away from the living room.

On every camera lens, a hand-painted red eye stared outward, as if placed by a fingertip. Eyes, everywhere. Unblinking and purposeful. A hand-drawn gaze created for a sightless house.

Colin reminded himself to breathe. "Is there anything in the kitchen?"

Bishop tipped their head, glancing over their shoulder. "Yeah, you should probably take a look."

He walked around the couch and touched the place between Bishop's shoulder blades, stepping around them. "Interesting . . ." Each syllable lingered. He crossed the kitchen and circled the table, studying two upturned crystal wineglasses, their narrow necks and spherical bases pointed toward the ceiling, their goblet mouths pressed to the wood, caging two eyes—one pupil shaped like a star, the other shaped like a scythe.

"I hadn't unpacked those," Bishop said. They cleared their throat, shifting their weight from one foot to the other. "They were wedding gifts. Handmade in Tuscany, I guess. Came with a fancy cabernet, but we just . . ." They paused, laughing under their breath. "We drank it straight from the bottle."

Colin tapped the base of a glass. "Your husband—"

"Ex-husband."

"Your ex-husband," Colin rectified, nodding carefully. "What happened?"

The roof pulled like a spine, crowding the old house into a small, significant space. Hardly hollow, blatantly watched, waiting for a confession. Everything felt contained. Taut and tightened, a fist ready to strike. Colin took each wineglass by the stem and flipped them upright.

"We grew apart," Bishop said. They took long strides across the kitchen and plucked the wineglasses off the table, placing them into the sink. Fished in the bottom cabinets, grabbed a dish towel, sprayed organic cleaner on the table, and scrubbed the paint or blood or ink away. "He wanted things I didn't; I wanted things he didn't. In the end, wanting each other wasn't enough."

"Will you tell me his name?" Colin asked.

Bishop stilled like a frightened animal. Their knuckles paled around the cedar-scented cleaning spray. "Lincoln," they said, hardly above a whisper, and cleared the emotion from their throat. "Lincoln Stone."

The house exhaled, trembling like an unsteady wing.

A door on the second story slammed. Heavy feet hit the staircase. Wind rushed, careening through the house, and gusted against Colin, twirling in the curtains, dying on a gasping, forceful breath. The sound echoed, shaking and shattering, and for a moment, Bishop's face crumbled. Their chin dimpled and their eyes watered, and Colin saw their heartbreak hemorrhage like a split vein.

"Bishop," he said gently, like he would to a bird. "Was that—"

"I can't," they said, swatting at their damp cheek and brushing past Colin. A rushed "*shit*" echoed in the hall, followed by something clattering on the floor, then stairs creaking under their feet. Seconds later, another door slammed upstairs.

Colin heaved a sigh and turned his gaze to the smooth ceiling. He held his hands out, palms open.

"Quite a show," he mumbled, shifting his jaw back and forth. "But despite the cameras and Bishop and whatever roots you've grown inside them, I've been hired to clean, and I *will* tear you out of this house."

The air turned. Fine hair on the back of Colin's neck stood on end, and a low, purring growl coasted into the space behind him. He felt the presence manifest. Icy energy. Chaotic, jittery vibrations. Predatory. Prideful. Completely, unerringly lovesick. He glanced at the transparent reflection on the glass slider.

"Hello," Colin said.

The wolf-headed creature snarled. "Get out, priest."

"Fortunately, I'm not a priest."

"You're not welcome here."

"Tell that to Bishop," he whispered, and turned on his heel, mouth open to speak. He exhaled, irritated, when he faced nothing but the absent air and the door leading to the basement, cracked and dark, on the other side of the room.

CHAPTER FIVE

C OLIN REVIEWED THE SURVEILLANCE FOOTAGE after eating an unfulfilling dinner—soggy Caesar salad, black-pepper chicken, and a lemon wedge. He picked iceberg lettuce from between his teeth and glanced out the guest bedroom window, watching frost spiderweb the shadowy glass.

Square boxes spanned his laptop screen. The time stamp ticked in the bottom corner, rolling forward through the previous night, into the morning, throughout the day. He watched the cameras fall from their perches—ripped out of their adjustable mounts and arranged throughout the house by invisible hands. In the top center square, the upstairs hallway was featured in grainy, greenish video, darkness shifting and bending until the recording switched from past to present. The fast-moving screen halted, and the time stamp slowed, seconds changing on the live feed.

Half-past midnight, he thought. *A cushion for the witching hour.*

Movement disrupted the calm screen. A door floated open. Bishop stepped out, swaying on their bare feet, and stepped into the hall. They tipped their face downward. Pulled at the webbing between their fingers and wrung their hands. Shuffled across the floor until they were positioned outside the bedroom.

Colin turned, watching Bishop's shadow hover at the bottom of the door, and closed his laptop, setting it carefully on the nightstand. Heat swelled in his chest, in his gut, *lower*, and he reminded himself to collect his desire. To lock away the want needling his pelvis, the strange excitement attached to the potential of Bishop, someone distant and dishonest, someone abrasive and beautiful, visiting him in the night.

He slipped out of bed and adjusted the drawstring on his joggers. Grasped the handle and tugged it open, revealing Bishop, pupils blown, lips parted with surprise, lingering awkwardly in the doorway.

"You're awake," Colin rasped, and cleared his throat. "I—I saw you on the camera. I thought you might be sleepwalking again—"

Bishop blinked, startled. "Oh, no. I'm . . . Yeah, I'm up." Their eyes scaled Colin's naked chest and their slender throat worked around a swallow. "I brought you here to clean my house, because I can't do it myself."

Colin squared his shoulders. "That's not uncommon. Most people don't know how to deal with the paranormal, supernatural, peculiar—whatever you'd like to call it."

"But some people do," Bishop said.

He nodded curtly. "Some people do."

The air thinned. Behind him, ice ghosted Colin's spine. Breath, suddenly there. The rumbling, ethereal sound of a growl crackling into existence. Before he could turn and face the apparition, Bishop extended their arm and shoved him sideways, revealing a wolfish maw and sharp, wet teeth.

"De las tinieblas vienes, de las tinieblas te vas," Bishop hissed. Their voice trembled, quickening on stunted breath. "Get out," they snapped. Power burst from them. Unrestrained, volatile *power*. Their eyes flared gold, pupils expanding outward over their sclera, and took a feline shape.

The wolf-man snarled and swung his arm in a sweeping arc. His palm cracked Bishop's cheek. Before Colin could step between them, Bishop whipped toward the wolf-man and shouted, "Lincoln, enough! De las tinieblas vienes, de las tinieblas te *vas!*" Primal power burst from them. Gold strung from their mouth and splattered on their chin like blood, imbuing each word with purpose. They heaved in another breath. "*Get out!*"

Like a riptide, Bishop's power, witchcraft, *something* yanked the wolf-man—*Lincoln*—into a different plane. Gold spun around his ankles, shaped like thread, and pulled him through the floor. His eyes widened and his jaw slackened, but all that was left of Lincoln Stone before he disappeared was the echo of Bishop's name, spoken like an apology.

Bishop breathed heavily. They stared at the place where Lincoln had faded, flexing their hands into fists at their sides. When they wiped the strange gold substance from their mouth, the back of their hand came away red. "Banishing spells only keep him away for a few hours. Sometimes a day if I'm lucky."

Colin stood on a tripwire. His muscles locked, and his knuckles paled, and he hardly knew what to do now that two of Bishop's secrets had collided before his eyes.

"You're a witch," he blurted, stupidly.

"Brujo," Bishop corrected, and glanced over their shoulder. "But yeah, more or less."

"Which is it—more or less?"

Their lips quirked halfway to a bitter smile. "More, I guess."

Colin gave them a slow once-over and narrowed his eyes. The truth turned Bishop jagged and severe, and he could not look away from them.

"This is the part where you explain what the fuck is going on," he said, and met their fierce gaze. "In great detail."

Bishop turned to face him. A sigh tumbled over their lips. They took a step, another, closing the small space between the two of them. "I will, but like I said, we only have a few hours."

Heat blistered in Colin's cheeks. "And?"

"And I've been trapped in a haunted house with the ghost of my ex-husband for six months." They didn't reach for his hand. Didn't test a touch to his arm or lick their lips. Instead, Bishop grabbed the drawstring on Colin's joggers like they'd done it a thousand times before, fingers secure on the smooth fabric, and tipped their head. "Am I reading this wrong?"

Colin almost reared back. Almost flattened his palm on Bishop's chest and gave a little push. That's certainly what he should've done.

"No, you're not," he said, too quietly, and swallowed to wet his rapidly drying throat. "But this is a terrible idea."

The pair stood before each other, posturing like birds of prey or venomous snakes, two creatures unused to the idea of being known, or seen, or held. Colin peeled his tongue off the roof of his mouth, flicking his attention from Bishop's face to their handsome hands, from their hands to their neck. *Beautiful*, he thought, *and dangerous.* When he met their eyes, they inched closer. Colin did nothing to stop them.

Bishop pulled the drawstring, loosening his sweatpants. "Yeah, I know," they said, and dusted their mouth across his chin. The playfulness emptied, leaving their voice raw and hopeful. "C'mon, exorcist. Don't make me beg."

Colin's blush worsened. The lamp on the nightstand sent shadows pouring across the floor, stretching away from ankles and streaking Bishop's fine-boned face. He tried to convince himself to step backward, to dislodge from their barely-there hold on him, but Bishop's honeyed eyes refused to let him go. Fingertips touched the place above his waistband, trailing his bare hip bones, and Colin couldn't fathom not kissing them. He framed their jaw with his thumb and pulled them to him, sealing their mouths together.

Bishop surged against him. They parted their lips, sending damp, hot breath across his teeth, and mapped his torso with their palms. Touched his belly button and the slight curve at his waist, followed the crescent scar beneath his pectoral, thumbed delicately at his ribs. Colin hoped they couldn't hear his wild heartbeat. Silently prayed to a deaf savior and asked for steady hands to hold them with. When they licked into his mouth, Colin stumbled backward, pulling Bishop with him, and when they scraped his lip with their teeth, he cracked his eyes open and met their hungry gaze.

"Where can I touch you?" Colin asked.

"I'm not picky—everywhere; anywhere." They guided his hands to the edge of their shirt and allowed him to peel the garment up and away. Their chest stuttered on unsteady breath, cheeks suddenly darker, hands suddenly shakier. "Believe it or not, I don't do this often."

"Sleep with the hired help?" Colin brought his hands to their small breasts, trailing their stomach and sternum, skimming their peaked nipples, and framing their neck with his wide hands.

Bishop didn't answer. They stared at Colin, gaze flicking from his long eyelashes to his parted lips. Without taking their eyes off him, they extended their arm toward the lamp.

"Ven a mi," they whispered, and flicked their fingers in a quick circle. Light darted from the bulb and sank into their palm, basking the room in darkness.

"What does that mean?" Colin asked.

They slid their hand into his joggers, warmed by stolen light. "Come to me."

Moonlight skirted the edge of the bed, spilling over tangled ankles. Colin watched Bishop's index finger trace the bold black ink etched into his chest, and rolled the lingering taste of them around in his mouth. Usually, Colin wandered into dive bars or swiped right on dating apps and met for one-night-stands with people who rarely asked his name, nonetheless his occupation. Whatever this was, it was rare and poignant. Fresh memories fit into pockets where bones met and bent: Bishop gasping through an orgasm with their nails deep in Colin's forearms, holding on to him while he held them against the bed. Their fingers between his legs, spit-slicked and buried inside him, and their bedroom-soft voice cutting through the shadow, whispering *you don't have to be quiet; let me hear you.*

"My grandmother was a healer," Bishop said, breaking the silence. "She worked in Mexico City for a while. Spent time in El Paso. No one ever called her a witch until she crossed the border and moved in with my mother and me. She'd always been a divine woman. Someone who could coax the colic out of a newborn, sing dying gardens back to life, borrow the glow from a streetlamp to light a prayer candle. She was blessed, you know."

"I'm guessing she's the one who taught you?" Colin asked.

"She died before she got the chance, but I studied her journals. Connected with a few of her friends at church and they showed me the ropes. I'd bet good money she's turning in her grave knowin' I joined the military."

"Why did you?"

Bishop pushed their face against the pillow. Their sleepy eyes gentled. "I was never a great student. Got in trouble as a kid, couldn't afford college, didn't know what else to do besides bag groceries or bartend, so . . ." They heaved a sigh. "The military came with benefits, salary, retirement, the works. It seemed like a solid option."

Colin listened, but his mind wandered. He wanted to put his teeth to Bishop's shoulder. Crawl down their body and bury his face between their thighs again. "Is that where you met Lincoln?"

They nodded. "He watched me sweet-talk a bullet out of someone's lung. It's hard to explain ancestral shit to some people. Hard to make *magic* sound less fairy tale and more spiritual. He understood, though. I should've clocked his willingness to *learn* and *be there* and *get me* right off the fucking bat, but I was too . . ." They walked their fingers across Colin's rib. "Relieved to be with someone to make myself pay attention."

"To what?"

"His obsession with the occult—ghosts, demons, parallel universes. I didn't mean to encourage it, but we practiced together sometimes, and when you're into something with someone, when you spend every single day with a person, you don't notice the shitty changes and new habits until it's too late."

"Shitty changes?"

Bishop furrowed their brow. "Scary changes."

"When you say *practiced together*, you mean—"

"Parlor tricks, really. Lighting candles, spirit board sessions, levitation." They paused, following Michael's angelic rune carved over Colin's heart. "I found a sigil on him one night. Handmade. Demonic; planetary. I thought it was bullshit, but . . ." They exhaled through a sour smirk. "It wasn't. Are these for show or do they really protect you?"

That was a question Colin had never been sure enough to answer. He stayed still, inhaling and exhaling, blinking slowly at Bishop with his cheek propped on the pillow. "Depends," he said. "Do you believe in God?"

"Like, *the* God or *a* God?"

"The biblical God."

"Sometimes, yeah. Recently, no."

"I was devout—I *am* devout."

"Hard not to be in your line of work," Bishop mumbled.

Colin took Bishop's hand and guided their fingers to the cross tattooed in the soft dent at the base of his throat. "But I made a mistake a long time ago, and I've been trying to earn my way back ever since."

"Way back to what?"

"To God, to faith, to believing in something bigger than myself. That's what this is, obviously. Cleaning houses, cleaning people." He resisted the urge to nip Bishop's finger when they brushed their thumb across his lip. Heat burned low in his abdomen, squeezing tightly, churning and grinding.

"What made you irredeemable, exorcist? Sex out of wedlock?" Bishop teased, the click at the end of *wedlock* popping in their mouth.

"Something like that," he said. *Nothing like that.* "What happened to Lincoln?"

Bishop rolled onto their back and turned their eyes to the ceiling. "Have you ever met someone who was afraid to die?"

"Isn't everyone?"

"I'll rephrase." They huffed out a sad laugh. "Have you ever met someone who wanted to be immortal?"

"I'm Catholic," Colin said matter-of-factly.

"Right." They sighed. "Well, Lincoln wasn't, but he was desperate to find eternity. He wanted to steal power, cheat death, free himself from earthly chains—*whatever*—and I didn't take him seriously. I mean, how could I?" They lifted their arms and dropped them beside their head. "But I found him cutting sigils into his thigh. Blood all over the bathroom, candlewax on the bed, wine spilled in the sink, and I knew right then, *right then*, I'd lost him. What the hell do you say to the person who's shared a house with you, built a whole goddamn life with you, and still managed to slip away?"

"You say goodbye," Colin whispered. He remembered being young, searching for purpose and hope, and finding the dead instead. Hunting for angels in empty places, praying to a God who didn't listen. Making mistakes. Ending a life.

They closed their eyes. "I put a knife in his chest."

Chills scaled Colin's arms.

Bishop continued. "Tried to stop whatever spell he'd started and bound him to the house, I guess. Or to me. Maybe I didn't bind him to anything, I don't know. But he's here—Lincoln, Marchosias, whoever he is now—and I don't . . . I *can't* get rid of him."

"Can't or won't?" Colin asked.

Bishop turned to look at him. "Does it matter?"

Colin heard the house take a breath. He kissed Bishop on the mouth, caged them against the bed and put his lips to their throat, the underside of their breast, below their bellybutton, and scooped his arms around their thighs. "You said a few hours, right?"

Their breath hitched, body arching into Colin's hands. "At least, yeah," they said.

Lying, again.

Colin didn't mind. *Let him see us, then*, he thought, and wrung pleasure from Bishop's tired, beautiful body. *Let him watch.*

CHAPTER SIX

MORNING RICOCHETED THROUGH THE FROSTED window, stained gray by a surprise storm. Snow flurries twirled through the air in the driveway, and warblers hunkered down in the naked tree in the yard. Colin glanced at the empty place beside him, touched two fingers to the dent in the pillow, and thought of Bishop's calf resting on his shoulder. Their bodies connected, rocking together in the witching hours.

He stripped the bedsheets and tossed them in the laundry basket. *Don't get attached.* Knuckled at his eyes. Grabbed a fresh set of clothes and walked to the bathroom.

He'd had his fair share of devastating romantic endeavors, but he'd never fallen into bed with a client before. Tipping his jaw, he stared at the half-moon bite mark on his shoulder. Bishop had certainly challenged his rules of engagement. Shattered them, really.

Colin raked his fingers through his mussed hair and scrubbed his palm over the buzzed area around his ears. Before he could reach for his toothbrush, the mirror rattled. He paused, hand hovering over the sink, and searched the reflection for abnormalities. There was nothing.

He hummed and rested his fingers on the glass. The name Bishop had used last night stayed fixed in the front of his mind. *Marchosias.*

Wolf demon. Hell hound. The creature Lincoln had channeled or offered residency to—someone, some*thing* deadly and wicked. He mouthed the name to his reflection and watched his eyes split, grow, concave, his face elongate, his teeth sharpen.

Lincoln Stone, whatever he'd become, rested his human fingertips against the backside of the mirror, melding together where Colin's corporeal form and Lincoln's ghostly presence met on the glass. Lincoln's feral face sprouted from the neatly folded collar on his suit shirt. Stoic and handsome, he gazed at Colin, assessing the exorcist with slow flicks of his canine eyes.

"You're brave," Lincoln said. Pointed teeth folded over his bottom lip. He didn't growl or snarl, but when Colin tilted his head, he followed the movement. "Their heart is a bear trap."

"I haven't seen their heart," Colin said. The half-truth slid past his lips like the beginning of a Hail Mary.

"Even priests lie."

"Are you Lincoln or are you Marchosias?"

A hand shot through the mirror and seized Colin by the throat. Lincoln pulled his muzzle into a fierce growl. Tightened his grip and fit his thumb beneath Colin's sloped jaw. "Keep our names out of your mouth."

"Ah," Colin wheezed, standing on his tiptoes, palms flattened on the counter to stay steady. "So we have an integration, then. *Daimonizomai*."

"*We* have nothing," Lincoln snarled.

"You know that isn't . . ." He strained against the unforgiving hold on his neck. "Exactly true."

"*I* have Bishop Martínez," Lincoln said, leaning until his snout rippled through the mirror. Hot breath gusted Colin's chin. "I live in them. I fill their bones like marrow. Their blood is my blood. You'll never clean this house, exorcist."

Colin gritted his teeth. He reached for the dormant power winding beneath black ink. "Michael, protector, Saint in the Armory, shackle this soul. Take this ruined spirit and cast it into eternal flame," he choked out, and wrenched away from Lincoln, snatching the wolf-man's wrist in a firm grip. "Arrest your fallen brother and deliver him back to the darkness—"

"Yes," Lincoln hissed, and craned toward Colin. "Spread your wings, brother. Fly to me."

Panic spiked through Colin's stomach. He tried to dodge, but Lincoln shot his hand out and gripped Colin's throat again, squeezing hard. This time, heat unfurled. Bit and blistered and boiled. Colin gasped, fumbling on the counter until his hand hit round beads tucked inside his toiletries bag. Pain ratcheted, blooming in patches where Lincoln's fingers cut grooves into his flesh. Colin fumbled with his rosary and slammed the crucifix against Lincoln's furry forehead, hardly inching past the mirror's distorted surface.

"Heavenly Father, hear me, your servant," Colin croaked.

Floorboards squeaked in the hall.

"Colin? It's, like, ten-thirty. You up?" Bishop called, voice sweet and curious. Their hand met the doorframe and a gasp tore through the bathroom. "*Lincoln!*" They crashed into the small space and clawed at Lincoln's arm. Their pupils elongated, eyes glowing bright and brutal. "Enough!"

The distraction lent Colin a breath. "I adjure thee, demon," he said, and funneled the energy humming in his runes toward the crucifix.

Lincoln lurched backward. He opened his jaws and a thousand voices poured out, screaming, howling, yelping, before he disappeared, blinking out of existence.

Colin caught himself on the sink. "*Jesus,*" he seethed. He reached for his throat but hesitated, fingertips quivering above scorched skin. His reflection stared back at him, cheeks blotchy with exertion, neck marred by a hand-shaped burn.

"Fucking . . . hell," Bishop whispered, taking Colin by the elbow. "C'mon, I'll make a salve."

"Your ex-husband is a menace," Colin said. He stumbled after Bishop, trailing them through the hall, down the stairs and into the kitchen.

"I'm aware." Bishop set their hands on his shoulders and leaned him against the table. "Sit."

"Was that a revenge throttle or has he always been this brutal?"

"He can be a little possessive," Bishop mumbled. They banged around in the kitchen, collecting palm-sized mason jars filled with herbs, gelatinous substances, and powders. A mortar and pestle clacked on the counter, and they went to work grinding seeds, scraping aloe leaf, and dumping raw honey into the stone bowl.

"I'll have you know, last night wasn't *my* idea." Colin aimed each word at the ceiling.

"Ay, Dios mío, don't taunt him," they bit out, angling their mouth over their shoulder.

Colin winced, tempting a light touch to his neck. The skin was singed and raw, warped, and reshaped. He squeezed his eyes shut and tried to focus on something, *anything* else, but the longer he sat there, the more intense the pain became. "Tell me about your eyes," he said.

"What about them?"

"They're quite catlike when you're magically charged."

"*Magically charged,*" they parroted, sounding out each syllable. "Apparently, my family was born from the Smoking Mirror. Tez-catlipoca, the Aztec God who governs the night sky, routinely wears jaguar skin on his hunts. According to my abuela, we're blessed by him."

"Peculiar," Colin said, and opened his eyes.

Bishop shuffled across the kitchen, cradling the mortar in one hand, and dipped their fingers into the bowl, collecting a glob of freshly churned salve. "Is it?"

"Not you—the circumstances," he clarified. "I'm rather skilled when it comes to sniffing out power, yet I didn't sense you. Your house? Yes. Lincoln? Yes. But not you."

Their cool, sticky fingers met his throat, laying soothing balm onto his wound. Colin winced. Stayed still. Sighed, relieved, when the sting started to subside. They set the mortar down, dug in the front pocket of their blue jeans, and pulled out a nickel-sized talisman. "I keep myself cloaked."

"A little ward," Colin said, humming softly. "I should've known."

"You were distracted."

He watched their lashes flick, studied the concentration tightening their face, and said, "Yes, I was."

Bishop dabbed salve onto his throat until the burn was completely covered. They framed the underside of Colin's jaw with their thumbs, closed their eyes, and mouthed words he didn't recognize. Gusty whispers danced on their lips. Gentle purrs and warm vowels floated into the air between the two of them, and Colin felt his wound begin to stitch and shut, pull and strengthen.

"It's not much, but it'll help," Bishop murmured, and opened their eyes, staring at Colin with gorgeous feline orbs. "Better?"

"Much," Colin said.

"Do you have a plan yet?"

"Are you telling me the entire truth yet?"

Bishop flicked their eyes around Colin's face, pupils shrinking and turning spherical, color darkening to forest brown. "Yeah." They cleared their throat. "I've told you everything."

"You haven't," he said, and pushed away from the table. He plucked two frosty beers from the fridge and knocked a chilled bottle against Bishop's hand. "Let's go outside."

"*Outside?* There's a storm happening. Like, immediately, right now."

"Rather endure the snow than deal with . . ." He circled his hand in the air. "Your murderous house."

Colin toed on his oxfords and trudged onto the porch, leaving shoeprints in the snow gathering on the walkway. He slipped into his car—a jet-black Subaru with California plates—and tipped the bottle against his mouth. The distinct, fizzy taste reminded him that it was hardly past morning. Bishop plopped into the passenger seat and shut the door, bundled in a throw blanket they'd taken from the couch on their way out. They turned toward Colin, half-swaddled, clutching their beer, and huffed.

"How, exactly, did you kill Lincoln?" Colin asked. "Assuming you *did* kill him."

Bishop drained half their beer in one go. "I stabbed him through the heart with a kitchen knife," they said, voice rasped by the alcohol. "He was attempting to summon Marchosias in our bedroom. I was supposed to help him. He . . ." They paused, glancing at the house as snow settled on the windshield. "He wanted me to cut him at a specific moment. Just enough to spill his blood onto a burning candle. I didn't . . . I didn't know what to do, so I just did what he asked and hoped it wouldn't work."

"And?"

"And Marchosias answered his call." They sipped their beer again.

Colin noticed the way their shoulders rounded toward their ears, how they guarded themself, withdrawing into the seat like a child. He inhaled a long, deep breath and licked his lips. "There's another way for me to get the information I need. It'll be quicker, but it won't be pleasant."

"Extraction," Bishop said morosely.

"You've done your research."

"I've seen my fair share of backyard exorcisms, Colin. I know what they entail."

"Extraction isn't always exorcism."

"Yanking my memories out into the open is a close enough comparison," they snapped, and finished their beer. "You said it'll be quick?"

"If you let me in, yes."

They wrinkled their nose. "Where . . . ?"

"Here is fine. Turn toward me, please," Colin said. He shifted in the driver's seat and opened his hands, cupping Bishop's warm jaw. He curved his thumbs in front of their ears, latched his fingers around their skull. "Relax, all right?"

"Easier said than done."

Carefully, Colin worked his thumbs along their temples, angling their face toward him. "Breathe. Think back to that moment."

Bishop met his gaze. They stared, unblinking, breathing deeply, before they finally closed their eyes and allowed Colin to sink into their mind. Power met and mingled. Bishop's wild, unruly magic shrank from Colin's manufactured sainthood, but he chased them into the shadowy recesses of their mind and latched on to their memories.

Candlelight flickered in his peripheral. He saw what Bishop had seen, felt what Bishop had felt—smooth, bare chest; legs straddling their lap; sleek pillar candle splattered with blood; half-filled goblet on the nightstand brimming red; Lincoln's voice, hitched and furious, calling for Marchosias. Panic shot through him, rippling outward from Bishop's memory, and Colin witnessed the moment Lincoln changed. Turned. Became a vessel for something worse. Lincoln tore the flesh from his face, clawing at his skin until it split, broke, came away like putty, and revealed the wolfish horror beneath. Bishop plunged the blade into Lincoln's chest. Their voice fluttered softly, the same way it had in the hall when they'd been sleepwalking. *I'm sorry.*

Everything muddied after that. Bishop's memories ran into each other, some new, some old. Lincoln kissing them on the mouth, breathing hard, moving like rough seas. Porcelain laughter. Champagne flutes clinking. Bishop holding on to Colin's face the night before, panting against his lips. Months ago, staring up at Lincoln's canine head, tracing the scar on his chest with two fingers, and the hot breach as his body pushed into theirs. A slick, black-handled kitchen knife dropping with a muted thud onto ruined bedsheets—

Colin tumbled backward out of Bishop with the last bit stamped behind his eyes: Bishop staring at their bloody hands and feeling across Lincoln's torso, trying to wake him. Bishop gasped and ripped away, smacking the back of their head against the passenger's window. Colin hissed and flattened the heels of his palms against his eyes.

"Ow—*fuck*. Okay, bad news, I might puke in your car," Bishop whined.

"Yeah, I forgot to mention that part," Colin mumbled and pointed lazily at the door handle. "Sometimes it's not—"

Bishop threw open the car door and emptied their stomach into the gutter.

"Okay, sometimes it *is* that bad," he corrected, sighing through his nose. "You okay?"

They sniffled, breathing slowly. "Go to hell."

"That's fair."

They dry-heaved again, then tossed their empty beer bottle into the gutter. Glass shattered and they stumbled onto the snowy sidewalk, dragging the blanket around their shoulders like a cloak. While they took heavy steps toward the porch, Colin finished his beer and dropped the bottle into the blue recycling bin against the curb.

Well, that went as poorly as possible, he thought. Granted, Bishop could've puked *in* his car, or kept them both trapped in an uncomfortable memory, or resisted completely, but instead, they'd opened like an abalone. Hard to crack at first, then too interesting to look away from. Colin scrubbed his upper arms and stepped onto the porch, staring at a snowflake caught in Bishop's eyelashes.

"He was your husband," Colin said, as gently as possible. The memory burned like a lantern—Bishop, lying bare beneath Lincoln's phantom form. "I don't judge you or your choices. I probably would've done the same thing."

"You were never supposed to *see* my choices," they barked. A furious blush darkened their face.

"Sometimes shame is a lesson. Most of the time, it's just a way for us to hate ourselves for the things we want."

They shifted their eyes to the door. "What do you know about shame?"

"I'm Catholic," Colin said matter-of-factly, and braved a touch to Bishop's knuckles.

They lingered for a moment. Allowed Colin to link his thumb around their fingers and stroke their palm. They dislodged quickly, though. Pushed through the door and disappeared up the stairs, bypassing a shadowy figure darting along the wall, and rounded the corner. A moment later, their bedroom door shut. Colin exhaled through an irritated sigh.

If Lincoln had summoned Marchosias—*integrated* with Marchosias—then what purpose did the crone and the other ghouls serve? Why fill an already occupied place with weaker spirits? To distract, maybe. To keep Bishop restless and spent.

Colin glanced from the stairwell to the ceiling, from the ceiling to the living room. In his frustration, he snatched at the air, catching a shadow by the ankle. One squeeze, two words—*be gone*—and the lost little thing fractured into pieces, disintegrating like ash in the air. The house tightened, lunglike and defensive, as another one of its tenants was forcefully expelled.

He stood in the foyer. Watched the hall closet float open. Rolled his eyes and hung his head, attempting to mentally scrub Bishop and Lincoln off the back of his eyelids.

Don't pry, he chided. *Don't fixate.*

Colin walked to the couch and sank to his knees, propping his elbows on a blank cushion. Extraction wasn't exorcism, but much like exorcism, extraction stayed with the excavator. Watermarked the searching presence with imprints from another person's heart.

Colin swallowed hard. "Hail Mary full of grace, the lord is with thee; blessed art thou amongst women . . ." He uttered the prayer swiftly, but couldn't chase the heat from his body, couldn't detach from the foreign memories, couldn't clear Bishop Martínez from his mind.

Bishop, reaching for Lincoln. Bishop, pressing their lips to Colin's sternum. Bishop covered in blood.

By evening, the electricity had given out, snow piled in the driveway and frosted the windows, and flames munched logs in the fireplace, illuminating the coffee table and the edge of the couch.

Colin sat cross-legged on the floor, stirring thick-cut bacon into his bowl of sharp cheddar macaroni. Bishop mirrored him, seated on a pillow with a blanket draped around their shoulders, dumping chili flakes into their noodles. The two of them hadn't spoken since the extraction attempt in Colin's car, and midday had come and gone with Bishop still locked in their bedroom.

At one point, Colin almost knocked on their door, but opted to trap himself in the shower instead, palms flat on the tile, ignoring the desire pooling in his groin, and said an Act of Contrition while hot water stung the handprint on his throat. Afternoon had slipped by while Colin studied demonology, and Bishop hadn't emerged until well after nightfall, banging around in the kitchen minutes before the blackout.

When he'd first arrived at the house on Staghorn Way, wanting Bishop had been easy and flippant. But having them had turned Colin into a ruthless, aching schoolboy, insatiable and unable to focus. His skin felt claustrophobic, constricting his bones and holding tight to his skeleton, amplifying all the places that were too open, too untouched, too blasphemous. For the first time in years, he yearned for someone.

Don't get attached, you fool.

"You're quite the cook," Colin said.

Bishop tipped their face upward. "It's noodles, cheddar, and bacon," they said suspiciously. "Nothing special."

"I watched you season cream with fresh garlic *and* fold in three different kinds of cheese. Accept the compliment."

They poked at their dinner. Tension filtered through the silence, disrupted by shifting silverware and the crackling fire. Outside, wind howled, sending glittery snow through the pitch.

"I know nothing about you," they said. When Colin glanced at them, he caught a distinct pinkness glowing on their copper cheeks. They pushed their glasses up their nose with a bent knuckle. "You've been in my head; you've been in . . ." They paused, clearing their throat.

"What do you want to know?" Colin asked.

"Tell me about your mistake."

He forked more macaroni into his mouth and chewed, considering the truth in comparison to something, *anything* else. It'd been a long time since Colin had told the story, even longer since he'd thought about that brisk morning six years ago with a sober mind. Lying would've been much, *much* easier.

"Liquor, first. If you wouldn't mind."

Bishop quirked their head and the blanket fell from around their shoulders. "Bourbon or mezcal?"

"Surprise me."

They shuffled into the kitchen, lighting their way with their phone's flashlight, and returned carrying two short glasses and a bottle filled with amber liquid under their arm. They poured a generous amount into both glasses and pushed one across the floor with their foot.

"Surprise," they said, feigning playfulness. "Are we sipping or drinking?"

Colin tipped the glass against his mouth and swallowed. He wiped his lips with the back of his hand and knocked the glass across the floor.

"Drinking, *then* sipping," he rasped.

Bishop nodded curtly, raising their eyebrows. They poured him another double shot. "Got it."

He adjusted on the floor and turned his gaze to the fire. Sent the bourbon swirling along the sides of the glass. Swallowed around the hot sting left in his throat and touched the rigid scab on his neck. Anxiety needled him, prickling on the underside of his skin, but he heaved a quiet sigh and nodded.

"I found God in a woman named Isabelle," he said. His voice almost cracked over her name. His tongue was unused to making the sound. "She was my first everything. I considered myself an exorcist back then. Trained with the church, followed my faith, worked with Isabelle to deliver innocent people from unholy circumstances . . ." He paused, allowing liquor to soak his bottom lip. The memory pulverized his heart. "Until a demon leapt from an eleven-year-old boy and landed inside her."

Hello, priest. Colin remembered her chapped lips spreading for an unfamiliar voice. *Your whore tastes like crushed figs. Like sex and cigarettes. I can smell her cunt under your fingernails.*

He sipped his drink. "I don't know if you've ever seen it, but possession happens quickly. One moment, Isabelle Washington was laughing with me in the car, listening to Critical Role, and the next she was tied to a chair, snapping her teeth like a crocodile. Her skin flaked, her voice faded, her hair came away in fistfuls. I worked on her for seven months—*seven months.*" He drained the rest of his drink and exhaled sharply. "And when I finally got her back, she was lucid for long enough to ask me to end it." *Please, Colin.* Her trembling voice beamed through his mind. Colin physically recoiled, wincing terribly. *Have mercy on me, darling. Deliver me.* He glanced at the tips of Bishop's fingers and heard a small clink as they leaned over and poured him more bourbon. "Thank you."

Bishop set the bottle down and lifted their own glass. "When you say *end it*—"

"I cut her throat," Colin said. Each word landed like a bullet. He rested the glass against his mouth, staring at the floor in front of Bishop's bent knees. "She died in a barn on a Sunday morning. Five-foot-six, ninety-eight pounds, eyelashes plucked, teeth loose, fingernails torn. I have . . ." His voice fractured and he cleared his throat. "I have a picture of her, if you'd like to know what she looked like before."

They furrowed their brow, lips parted, wide eyes searching his face. Their throat flexed. "If you don't mind."

Colin swiped his finger across his phone and opened the photo app, scrolling until he found the lonesome folder at the bottom of a long list. He hovered over the first of several images. Swallowed around the sea urchin in his throat. Tapped the picture and turned the phone around, displaying Isabelle Washington in the passenger seat, window down, brunette hair roped into a loose braid, gold-framed sunglasses glinting in the summer sunshine. She was grinning, one finger hooked through the chain around her neck, crucifix dangling over her thumb.

Despite the whipping storm and the crowded, watchful house, Colin and Bishop fell into a shared silence. Bishop craned forward, blinking at the image of Isabelle. Colin buckled under the weight of missing her. Her absence hollowed him. Stayed with him. Haunted him. He swiped his thumb across his watery lashes and set his phone face down on the floor, tucking her smile away.

"I failed her, and I failed God," Colin said simply. He chewed on his tingling lip and let the alcohol rushing through his veins shoo the pain from his heart. "So I distanced myself from the Vatican and worked alone after that. Cleaning people and their houses, joining camera crews at active sites, bartering with angels for a chance at borrowed power. Exorcism stopped being a practice and became a tool."

Bishop tilted their head, bourbon-flushed and bathed in bouncing firelight. "You barter with angels?"

"Yes. Your power is ancestral, mine is permitted. My tattoos are protection, but they're also direct links to the High Court. The only reason I can banish and extract is because God's first creation allows it."

"And you think *God* won't listen?"

Colin pursed his lips. "God stopped listening six years ago."

They ran their mouth across the edge of their glass, sipping gingerly. Their bare feet stretched, and the blanket scooped around their shoulders, exposing the round neck on their thin sweatshirt. They took their glasses off and cleaned both lenses with the blanket. Quiet settled again. Snow fell, ghosts eavesdropped, and Colin wanted nothing more than to scream. *Give her back to me. Give him back to them.* But Isabelle was gone, and Lincoln had made his choice.

"You lied to get me here," Colin said.

Bishop lifted their gaze. "Yeah, I did."

"Why, though? Why carry a talisman to hide your magic? Why pretend not to know who's possessing your home? Why lie to the person investigating your entire life . . . ?"

They lifted their brows, watching Colin skeptically. "I murdered my husband," they said, leaning into each syllable. "I had no idea if you were a snake oil salesman, an undercover cop, or the real fuckin' deal. You showed up at my door, a clean-cut white guy carrying a briefcase, and I'm supposed to pour my fuckups at your feet? No, that's not how I operate."

"Was sleeping with me a test?" Colin dared.

"No, sleeping with you was selfish," Bishop snapped. Their flush deepened and they tossed back the rest of their drink.

Colin flopped backward onto the wood floor and heaved an exhausted sigh. He stared at the tippy ceiling, warm and pleasantly numb and too drunk to be angry or heartsick or any of the things he'd felt for the past few days.

"Well, you're an excellent lover," he blurted, accidentally, and blinked at the white paint. "And I certainly wouldn't call you *selfish*."

Laughter hiccupped in Bishop's throat. "I'm not sorry for lying to you."

"I'm not sorry for fucking you," Colin said.

Another laugh brightened the dark, chilly house. "Good."

"I think I know what to do."

Bishop pushed their toe into the sole of Colin's foot. "Yeah?"

Colin rested his cheek on the floor and stared at the staircase. A wolf peered through the banister's bars. Animal eyes glowed, tall ears twitched, but human hands gripped the stairs, long fingers and bent knuckles and trimmed nails. They looked at each other for a long time, or no time at all. Either way, when Colin blinked, Lincoln—Marchosias—was gone.

CHAPTER SEVEN

"A BOX," BISHOP DEADPANNED, STARING AT Colin from the driver's seat in their truck. Their breath fogged the air trapped inside the cab and their lithe body was wrapped in a thick quilt. "You're joking, right?"

Colin furrowed his brow. He smoothed his thumb along the rusted hinge and traced the Latin etched into the lid.

"Crafted from scraps left behind from the tool that decapitated Paul the Apostle," he said, and shot Bishop a tired glare. Last night, he'd fallen asleep on the floor with his back to the fireplace and woke with a blanket draped over him and a sweatshirt bundled under his cheek, nursing an inconvenient headache. Bishop's kindness hours ago did nothing to quell the annoyance Colin felt right then. He narrowed his eyes. "It's an empty *holy* box, obviously," he clarified. "It's typically used to usher wayward angels out of purgatory. We'll be using it to contain Marchosias, though."

"Oh, right. So we're trapping Marchosias, a Marquis of Hell, who is definitely *not* an angel, inside an angelic *elevator* box." They arched an eyebrow. "Great," they piped. "Awesome. Perfect. Sounds like a foolproof plan."

"*You* hired *me*, remember?"

Bishop flared their nostrils and pulled the quilt tighter around their shoulders. "How, then? How do we stuff a demon into a box when it's attached to someone's spirit?"

"Integrated," Colin said thoughtfully.

"What?"

"Integrated, not attached. An attachment is a non-oppressive bond formed with a deity. Integration is willful possession—submission, more or less."

They inhaled deeply and flapped their lips on an exhale. "So Marchosias and Lincoln share a soul . . . ?"

"Not quite. In life, they shared a body. In death, they share . . ." He paused, staring at the porch over snow clumped on the windshield. What *did* Lincoln and Marchosias share? The body they'd used was gone. All the two of them had left was a tangled, messy soul and an old house. He clenched his jaw, teeth gritted hard. "Well, you're right," he said, huffing. "We can't use the box, because Lincoln isn't an angel and he's barely a damn . . ." He dropped the empty box into his lap and raked both hands through his hair. ". . . *demon.*"

Bishop clucked their tongue. "No, he isn't," they whispered. "Lincoln bled like the rest of us whether he liked it or not."

I fill their bones like marrow. Their blood is my blood.

Colin blinked through the bourbon-soaked fog still clouding his thoughts. He recalled Lincoln's snarling snout growling each word. How the wolf-man had lunged through the mirror and seized his throat. Colin touched the collar-shaped scab ringing his neck, further in healing thanks to Bishop's spelled salve, and sighed through his nose. He remembered sifting through Bishop's memories, feeling what they felt, seeing what they'd seen.

"I have an uncomfortable question to ask you," Colin said.

"Of course you do. Shoot, I guess."

"There was a wineglass on the nightstand the night you killed Lincoln."

"Yes?"

"Your blood wasn't—"

"No, *Jesus Christ*, c'mon," Bishop yowled. They tried to swat him, but Colin recoiled against the passenger's door. "You think I'd perform *blood* magic with him? Really? *Seriously?* Do you honestly believe I'd . . ." They stopped, lips parted, tongue pressed to the roof of their mouth, and went still. Their throat clenched around a slow swallow, and their eyes flicked back and forth, glancing from Colin to the windshield. When they spoke, their voice hardly surfaced. "Why're you asking?"

"Did he drink your blood?" Colin asked.

"Tell me why."

"*Did he?*"

"Colin!"

He grunted, annoyed, and gestured to the house with a flat palm. "If he consumed your blood in a ritualistic or performative sense then he could very well be using you as a link to this plane. You'd be like his personal ley line, funneling earth-based energy into the spiritual realm, allowing him to live in both spaces."

Bishop thinned their lips into a pale line. Their eyes softened, falling to Colin's lap. They stared through him, lost in thought, absently touching the crease of their hip. A minute went by, then two, before they scoffed. Swiped at their glassy eyes and shifted their jaw back and forth, working through anger or hurt or a combination of both.

"Bishop," Colin tested, turning in his seat to face them. "What happened?"

They didn't move or breathe or blink. They shrank, almost, and Colin remembered seeing them for the first time, thinking *like a rab-*

bit. He touched the top of their wrist, but when their lips wobbled open, no sound followed. Another strained moment passed, then Bishop made a defeated noise, grasped Colin's hands, and brought his palms to their face.

Colin braced for another brutal extraction, but this time Bishop welcomed him. Opened easily and allowed him to look at the memory cycling behind their eyes. Skin against skin. Bishop's soft, cooed whimpers, their knuckles buckled in white sheets, breathless and panting, arching against the fingernails sinking into their hip. Colin followed Bishop's memory, lived through the moment they'd looked down at Lincoln's coy smile, and felt his tongue on their hip, lapping at the blood beading in the groove he'd raked across their flesh. Colin shied away, exiting Bishop's mind as gently as he could.

"Oh," Colin whispered. He leaned across the empty center seat, still clutching Bishop's face, and followed their cheekbones with his thumbs. "When—"

"Right before the . . . the inception, integration, *whatever . . .*" They opened and closed their mouth. Their pupils ate the color in their eyes. "Do you think—"

"Yes, he absolutely did it on purpose."

Bishop winced, and Colin wished he would've lied.

"I'm sorry," he said.

"Don't be."

They didn't pull away. Just stayed still, one hand wrapped around Colin's wrist, the other braced on the center seat. "What does it make me if I miss him?" they asked.

"Human," Colin said.

They breathed a little easier. "What now?"

"Plan B," he mumbled, and reminded himself to look away from Bishop's lips. "Have you ever heard of the Lazarus effect?"

"Isn't it a movie?"

"A stupid movie, yes. But it's a technique too."

Bishop released his wrist and sat back, easing out of his tender hold. "Explain."

"The Book of John recounts a man—Lazarus of Bethany—who had fallen ill and died—"

"Oh my God, Colin. I'm Mexican," they blurted, gesturing wildly to themself. "I'm half-Catholic by design. Skip the goddamn gospel. What's the technique?"

Colin narrowed his eyes. "I can't exorcise an entire house, especially when Marchosias has thrown open the door for lesser demons and peculiarities. But I could properly exorcise a smaller vessel."

"Smaller?"

"Body-sized."

"Body-sized," Bishop repeated, too loudly.

"I'm guessing you've never robbed a grave," Colin said. He flashed a pained smile. "Specifically, your ex-husband's grave."

"You want to raise my ex-husband from the dead?" Their words rushed together, clashing like a car wreck. "That's the Lazarus effect? *Necromancy?*"

"Clearly, you don't know the story—"

"I know the story," they bit out, and threw themself against the seat.

"He does have a body, doesn't he? If he was cremated, we can use someone else, but usually the ritual works best with the original host."

"He's buried in the Gold Hill cemetery two towns over. But have you . . . Have you ever done this before?"

"No, and I usually wouldn't consider it a viable option."

"That's comforting," Bishop said. They wound the quilt around the bottom half of their face. "What makes it *viable* now?"

"Lincoln bound himself to you moments before he integrated with a demon, which, to no one's surprise, prevents an exorcism. If I cut Marchosias away from Lincoln, Marchosias would simply hop into the closest conduit for power—you—and if I managed to control Marchosias for long enough to banish him, Lincoln would still have a tether to this plane. If we trap Lincoln and Marchosias in a human body, you'll have the chance to break your bond with Lincoln and I'll have the means to get rid of them both."

"Too many words," Bishop mumbled, pawing at their eyes.

"Anyway, I'll rephrase. It's not exactly viable, but it's somewhat doable."

"Awesome, great. Love the confidence," Bishop muttered, massaging their temples. "Where do we start?"

"I have most of the supplies, but we need rope, more candles, dead bolts."

"Dead bolts?" Bishop quirked their head.

"Once we secure Lincoln and Marchosias in a body, we'll need to secure them in a room."

"The basement has an old-school slide lock."

"Good. The dead bolt won't be hard to attach, then," he said, and opened the passenger's door, landing with a *crunch* in the snow. "We'll also need assistance with the other unwelcome guests residing in your house."

"*Assistance?*"

"Assistance," Colin said again, and glanced over his shoulder, sweeping his gaze across Bishop, wrapped and burrowed in their oversized blanket, wearing dark circles behind their glasses and an uncomfortable frown. "Get dressed. We'll stop for dinner too."

Moon Strike Nursery appeared far stranger after nightfall than it did during the day. The greenhouse was a dark, steady globe behind the repurposed cottage, and neon signs flashed in the icy windows. open shone bright pink, and beside it, a palmistry hand glowed above psychic in teal cursive. Colin pushed his nose into the striped scarf wrapped around his neck, concealing his marred skin and tucked neatly into the front of his coat. He tracked a silhouette moving beyond the glass, tidying shelves, arranging merchandise, flipping lazily through a book at the counter.

"Does she know you're a witch too?" Colin asked.

Bishop toed at the slick asphalt with their chunky boot. "I'm sure she knows I'm something," they admitted, and shrugged. "You really think she'll be useful?"

"She knew I was a cleaner the minute she saw me, and I knew she was a witch the minute I saw her. Awareness is a learned thing, so yes, I think she'll be useful. Helpful at the very least."

"And if she isn't?"

"Then we've wasted an hour. C'mon." Colin took the three rickety stairs to the covered porch and stomped stubborn snow from his boots. He stepped inside, greeted by a pleasant bell chime, and held the door for Bishop.

Faerie lights glinted around bookshelves. Calcite-speared soil in potted plants. Tehlor leaned her hip against the cash-wrap, snapping her teeth at a chewing gum bubble. She licked her lips, laughed under her breath, and toyed with a satin-wrapped piece of hair nestled in her yellow mane.

"How's your mess, honey?" she asked, jutting her chin toward Bishop.

Bishop pushed their hands into the pockets of their sheepskin flannel. "Messier," they said, glancing from Colin to Tehlor. "I think I need something stronger than a cleansing bundle."

"Well, you've got yourself a cleaner." She slid her attention to Colin. "Or is he a tad bit out of his comfort zone?"

"I'm perfectly situated, thank you. But we do require the help of a modern mystic," Colin said. He plucked a tchotchke rose quartz skull from a crowded shelf and turned it over in his hand. "You wouldn't know anyone, would you?"

"If you're looking for a mystic, ring the yoga studio down the street. If you're looking for a witch . . ." She trailed her banded fingers over a tall fiddle-leaf fig and came around the counter, straightening incense sticks in a narrow, upright display. Her eyes transferred from Colin to Bishop, Bishop to Colin. "I know a few. What's the job?"

"We'd like to shoo some spirits," Colin said.

Bishop stood beside a table filled with tumbled stones in various oblong bowls, awkwardly rocking on their heels, attention flitting from one place to the next. They cleared their throat. Fidgeted with polished labradorite pebbles and jasper flat stones.

Tehlor fixed Colin with a suspicious smile. "You can't handle a few ghosts?"

Witches. Colin's small smile tightened. *Arrogant as the devil.*

"Not these ones," Bishop said. They tossed a smooth, shiny onyx into the air and caught it. "I can pay you."

She laughed, a single, egotistical *hah.* "How 'bout this," she purred, folding her arms across her chest. Her ankle-length shawl drooped over her shoulder, revealing another wave of red ink breaking across her light ochre skin. "I'll come sniff out whatever dust bunnies you two can't seem to chase away, and you let me keep whatever I find. That'll be payment enough."

"Keep . . . ?" Bishop furrowed their brow.

"For Níðhöggr," she said. Her throat worked around familiarity, stretching open for deep, round sound.

Ice shot down Colin's spine. *No* leapt to his lips, but he clamped his mouth shut and turned his back to Tehlor, pretending to browse a cramped row of books. *Harnessing Magick, The Old Way, Lewellyn's Kitchen Witchery.* His throat turned to sandpaper. It'd been a long time—years, really—since he'd stumbled upon a Norse witch, and he hadn't expected to find one in Gideon, Colorado. He drew a careful, steady breath and set the pink skull on the shelf where he'd found it.

"I prefer to release," Colin said. He spun around, feigning a smile.

Tehlor hummed. "Sure you do, holy man," she rasped, smothering another laugh. "And yet you're here, asking for my help instead of *releasing* your pesky spirits. Take my offer or find someone else."

"What do you mean *keep?*" Bishop asked, their forehead tensed with confusion.

"She intends to trap the misplaced energy living in your home and use it to sacrificially power her spells," Colin said. He straightened his spine, staring at Tehlor down the slope of his nose. "Unfortunately, her deities require payment."

Tehlor shrugged one bony shoulder. "All gods require payment," she said. Her eyes fell to Colin's chest where his rosary sprouted from beneath his scarf. "Especially yours."

There was little Colin could do to argue that. He cataloged her slipper-shoes and torn jeans, the crystal jewelry around her neck and the Scandinavian tattoos scrawled across her skin. In a sense, she was right. He remembered Isabelle straining against the ropes tied around her wrists and ankles, shackling her to a rickety chair. How the light had left her eyes, and day by day, her soul had chipped away, weathered like an old building in an unforgiving climate. Love hadn't saved her. Sacrifice hadn't saved her. Christ hadn't saved her. For years, Colin had tried to find truth in God's plan, desperately searched his heart for grace and forgiveness. But faith was a hard, mean, vengeful thing at times, and losing her had calloused him.

"It's not my house," Colin said. He turned his attention to Bishop and waited.

Bishop set their mouth, shifting their jaw back and forth. Rhythmic trance flitted through the shop, thick wicks popped on rustic candles, and their damp boots squeaked on the clean floor. They met Colin's eyes and tipped their head, defeated, before aiming a curt nod at Tehlor.

"Are you free tomorrow?" they asked.

Tehlor pulled her mouth into a sly smile.

"I'll bring Starbies," she said, popping her lips. Her nautical eyes flashed between Colin and Bishop. "Anything I should know?"

"Are you a dog person?" Bishop asked, dryly.

"Are there people who aren't?" Tehlor laughed. Confusion moved across her face.

"Be cautious and vigilant," Colin said. He nudged Bishop with his elbow and made for the door, glancing over his shoulder. "Since you're bringing coffee, I assume you'll arrive in the morning?"

She nodded. "Send your address through the contact form on Moon Strike's website. I'm the only one with access."

"Will do," Bishop said. They followed Colin into the cold. At the truck, they snatched his forearm, tugging him around. "So we're letting a witch play animal control in my house? She's seriously going to trap the ghosts, phantoms—*whatever*—and keep them? Like, in an aquarium? In a trash bag? How the hell do people cage a non-corporeal being?"

"From my understanding, every witch and practitioner has their own standards when it comes to creatures outside this plane of existence. She's a Norse witch, and I'm betting ritual sacrifice still plays a major role in her life. The name she used, Níðhöggr," he said, wrinkling his nose at the clumsy pronunciation, "is a corpse-eating serpent. If I had to guess, I'd say she intends to impress him with whatever loot she catches at your house."

They pulled their slack jaw shut. "And you're okay with this?"

"Do we have another choice?"

"We could release them one by one. You said you've taken care of the crone, right? We'll handle the rest before we move forward with the Lazarus spell—"

"Lazarus effect."

"Whatever—it's fuckin' necromancy. Anyway, then we can handle Lincoln and Marchosias."

Colin leaned against the truck. "Have you ever released a spirit before?"

"I've seen it done."

"That's not what I asked."

They scraped their bottom lip with their teeth. Pride tightened their mouth into a pinched frown, and they stayed stubbornly silent.

"Releasing one spirit? Fine. But your current tenants have kept us awake for days. Sleeplessness equals weakness, weakness equals a longer recovery time for your magic and my power, and a longer recovery time allows Marchosias to kick the spiritual door wide open and invite more wanderers into your house. We need help, Bishop."

"From a Viking witch," they grumbled.

"Give me another option and we'll take it."

Their breath plumed the air. "Yeah, I know."

"What sounds good for dinner?" He wanted to reach for their hand.

Bishop blinked. He anticipated an argument, but thankfully, they sighed and shrugged. "Chili verde," they said. "There's a hole-in-the-wall taqueria downtown. Cheap margaritas, free chips and salsa."

"Done," Colin said, and slid into the passenger seat.

Vibrant picado banners drooped in arches from the ceiling at Cocina De León. Heat from the kitchen filled the small dining room, and Colin watched Bishop sip gingerly from a salt-rimmed margarita. They followed a soccer game playing on the flat-screen mounted in the corner, pupils dilated in the low light, and fingered through the basket of chips centered on the table.

"So what brought you to Gideon?" Colin asked, attempting to make conversation after the awkward exchange at the metaphysical shop.

Bishop crunched an ice cube. "We wanted a fresh start after being overseas. My mom works at a bakery in Austin, so I know she's secure, and Lincoln wasn't close with his family—didn't care to rebuild burned bridges. Gideon came cheap, felt cozy, had a small-town vibe with access to a nearby city. Just made sense." They glanced away from the game and settled their gaze on Colin's face. "Where are you from?"

Colin scooped chunky salsa onto a chip and popped it into his mouth. "Little desert town called Temecula in Southern California. Vineyards, wineries, and churches, mostly."

"Sounds bougie," Bishop said. They sighed through their nose. "Sometimes I miss home. The people, the food, the heat."

"Doesn't it get warm here?"

"Summer, yeah. But nothing like Texas. I used to smack the bottom of my boots to shake out scorpions. Used to be tan too," they said, rolling their sleeve to their elbow.

Colin dragged his milky fingertips along their wrist. "You're still tan."

"Compared to you, maybe," Bishop mumbled, lips tipped into a shallow smile. "Can't say I don't like this little mountain town, but . . ." They shrugged and lifted their fingers to brush Colin's palm. "I miss blazing afternoons, backyard cookouts, and plastic kiddie pools."

"You visit, don't you?" He played with Bishop's hand, tangling and untangling their fingers, dusting his knuckles across their pulse, trailing his pinkie along the blue vein striping their skin. Like this, Colin wondered about loneliness, how houses longed for occupancy and hearts yearned to be held.

They nodded. "Not as much as I should, but yeah. Do you have family in California?"

Colin stilled. His fingers framed Bishop's palm like an arachnid, caging their hand against the table. They traced his heart line. Stroked the webbing at the base of each digit.

Most people never asked about his family. Clients typically shied from the topic, colleagues were few and far between, and romantic conquests hardly lasted longer than a night. He cleared the tightness from his throat.

"I do," he said, allowing the statement to linger. "My sister and I usually get together for Thanksgiving or Christmas. I text my mother, but we aren't particularly close. My father and I haven't spoken in twelve years."

Bishop's mouth shaped the word—*twelve*—before they blinked, nodding slowly. "I'm sorry."

"No need to be," he said, and pulled his fingers across their palm, concealing his twitchy hands in his lap. A server dropped their plates at the table, chili verde for Bishop, tortilla soup for Colin. He squeezed lime into his steaming bowl and stirred. Kept his eyes on the shredded chicken and reddish broth, and tried to dismiss Bishop's eyes, flicking curiously around his face, prying at him.

"Did they know Isabelle?"

Hearing her name in someone else's mouth caused Colin's heart to squirm. "Rebecca did, yes."

"Your sister?"

Colin nodded. "Did your mother know Lincoln?"

"Yeah, she loved him," they said. "Thought he was a good one."

"Was he?"

They paused, forking pork and avocado into their mouth. "In the beginning, maybe. But I don't know if I can say I ever *knew* him."

"You loved him," he said.

"I loved who he allowed me to see," Bishop said. They focused on their dinner, sipping, chewing, dunking tortilla chips, and met Colin's eyes with a brief, sad smile. "Deception, dark magic, demonology. Typical marital problems."

"I can't imagine what you've been through. I've never married, but I do know Lincoln loved you," Colin said. He hoped he hadn't overstepped. Hadn't pressed his thumb to a softened scab. "I feel it in the house, I feel it . . ." *On you.* ". . . in his anger, his desperation, his loneliness."

Bishop rolled their lips together. Their brows tensed, shoulders pulling toward their ears.

"Love is supposed to be indomitable," they said under their breath. Someone scored during the soccer game and the speakers roared with cheers and music. A red-cheeked man clapped at the bar. Bishop turned toward the television. "But it's a ghost too. Still there, yeah. Still trapped in us. Just incorporeal. Gone, now."

Colin didn't know what to say to that. He thought of Isabelle and wanted to say *yes*, wanted to say *no*. He tapped the point of his shoe against Bishop's shin beneath the table.

"You don't mind staying for another drink, do you?" Bishop asked.

Colin shook his head. "No, I'm fine. We can stay for a while."

"Good." Bishop ordered another margarita. They took their time eating. "Because I don't want to go home yet."

Colin touched his toe to Bishop's shin again. *I know the feeling*, he thought. They linked their boot behind his ankle, swaying their shoes back and forth.

CHAPTER EIGHT

C OLIN DIDN'T SLEEP.

Leftover storm clouds spat snow and hail, and time warped throughout the night. After Colin and Bishop had finished their dinner, they stood together in the cold, watching their breath fog the air, and mist bend the light beneath a streetlamp. He'd imagined pressing Bishop against the wall in the alley attached to Cocina De León. Crowding them against the brick and asking them to swallow the yellow glow humming inside the lamp, kissing them hard and tasting magic on their lips. But he'd turned his gaze upward instead. Studied the starless sky and fixated on the place where Bishop's shoulder touched his own.

Back at the house, Bishop had glanced at him and disappeared into their room, and Colin had paced in the guest bedroom, chewing his fingernails and scolding himself for wishing he'd reattached the cameras. He'd never watched a client before. Never had the urge to invade someone's privacy, never wondered about the way unfamiliar bedsheets might wrap around ankles and pool over shoulders. But he wondered about Bishop. About their body stretched beneath blan-

kets, and their face suspended in peaceful sleep, and what he might do
to keep them awake.

Time had shifted again, sped and slowed. Colin woke after dozing,
dipping in and out of a dream about Isabelle, her ruined lips and
sallow eyes, her piano-key rib cage and nightmarish voice. He'd remembered seeing midnight blink on his phone, then two o'clock, then
four thirty, and couldn't recall how he'd lost the hours in between.
Maybe he'd slept. Maybe he'd touched himself. Maybe he'd sinned and
prayed and hoped Bishop would come to his room again.

Exhaustion sank bone deep. He pawed at his face, listening to the
quiet unravel as the blue hour bled into morning. He'd cleaned many
houses, exorcised plenty of people, but he'd never lost his senses to a
place before. Bishop's home seemed to be taking its toll—made him
unsteady on his feet, caused his thoughts to turn soupy and thin. He
groaned, rubbed sand out of his eye, and fished his toiletries bag out
of his suitcase, prepping a syringe with his weekly hormone dose. The
needle pinched, like always, and red beaded on his hip, like always,
darkening a permanent bruise splotched on his fair skin. He stored
the used needle in a plastic disposal case and brushed his teeth in the
hallway, dipping into the bathroom to spit and rinse before shying
away from the mirror again.

Bishop opened their bedroom door and snared Colin in a quizzical
look. "Why are you standing in the hall?"

He gestured lazily to the healing burn on his throat. "Last time, this
happened," he slurred, sucking foam off his toothbrush.

"Right." They scrubbed their palm over their buzzed head. "Get
any sleep?"

Colin laughed in his throat. "Hardly. You?"

"A few hours, maybe."

"What time is it?"

"Early. Almost seven," they said. Bishop propped their shoulder against the wall and met Colin's gaze, standing in their flannel sweatpants and long-sleeved shirt. They straightened their glasses. "Tehlor'll be here in a bit."

Colin nodded. "Do you happen to like McDonald's?"

"Everyone likes McDonald's, Colin," Bishop said patiently. "Whether they admit it or not."

"Can't argue with that. I'd offer to make something, but I'm a dreadful cook."

"Dreadful," they hummed, laughing under their breath.

"Simply *awful*." He turned his phone around and displayed the delivery app. "What would you like?"

"Two Egg McMuffins and a hashbrown," they said. Their smile curved crookedly on their handsome face. "Thanks."

He shooed the flapping in his chest—*relax, you idiot*—and disappeared into the bathroom. He'd seen every inch of Bishop's body, yet something as simple as breakfast after a sleepless night sent Colin whirling through teenage-era anxiety. Bishop's footsteps faded as they walked into their bedroom. Dresser drawers opened, hangers scraped the closet bar, and Colin almost tripped in the hall when he glimpsed Bishop through the open doorway, tugging underwear over their knees, shimmying lace-trimmed cotton into place.

Get a hold of yourself, he thought, and ducked into the guest room to get dressed. He wore crimson corduroy pants and a cream-colored turtleneck. Straightened his rosary, raked texturizer through his hair, smoothed moisturizer onto his face and hoped hydration might brighten his tired complexion. Still, every movement felt weighted, like he was swimming through molasses.

"Did you see anything last night?" Bishop asked. They waited for Colin to step into the hall. Their shoulder knocked his on the staircase, knuckles brushing, elbows bumping.

Colin glimpsed their mismatched socks and smiled. "No, but I did *feel* strange. Could've been the restlessness, but I . . . I don't know how to explain it, honestly. I lost hours. Slept, woke, slept, woke."

"What kept waking you?" Bishop asked.

You. "I'm not quite sure."

The house was unusually quiet. Biding time. Waiting. Colin glanced at the ceiling and startled, embarrassingly, at the *ding* of the doorbell. Bishop shot him a playful glare and opened the door to Tehlor, standing on the welcome mat, carrying a woven basket filled with mason jars and a tray stacked with to-go coffees. A beady-eyed rat perched on her shoulder. Beside her, the petrified delivery person leaned away from twitching whiskers.

"There's napkins in the bag," the Takeout Today employee said as they shoved the McDonald's bag at Bishop, then speed-walked to their car.

Tehlor smiled. "Mornin', honey," she said, before leaning onto one foot to peek at Colin. "Sorry, honey*s*."

Colin cleared his throat. "Good morning."

She stepped inside and toed off her winter boots. Her pale-yellow hair was bundled atop her head and tied with a velvet scrunchie. Crystals hung at odd lengths around her neck—tourmaline snug against her throat, celestite centered on her chest, smoky quartz nestled between her breasts. She pushed her rose-tinted sunglasses to the top of her head and assessed the house. As she turned her head, the rat on her shoulder turned, and when she blinked, the rodent blinked too.

"Wow," she sang. Her warm, raspy voice carried. "You weren't lying; it's loud in here."

"Extremely," Colin said.

Bishop tipped their head from side to side, considering. They unwrapped a McMuffin and took a bite. "Hopefully a little quieter after you're done," they said, one cheek stuffed.

"Oh, *much* quieter," she said.

Colin stood beside Bishop in the archway dividing the living room from the kitchen. He neatly unwrapped his sausage and egg McMuffin, attempting a relaxed appearance. Underneath his faux-calm exterior, his muscles tightened, and his stomach turned, and he silently recited an Act of Contrition.

Tehlor moved with purpose. She set the basket down and pinched a folded cloth between her fingers, spreading it over the floor. It might've been white once, but now it was stained like a swamp, flecked dark brown and creased with permanent wrinkles. Colin watched her. Followed each flick of her wrist. Paused mid-nibble of his muffin as she unsheathed a white-handled knife and plucked the rat from her shoulder.

"What's she . . ." Bishop dropped their McMuffin and plastered their hand over their mouth, smothering a gasp.

Colin winced.

The Norse witch drove the tip of her blade beneath the rat's small chin, detaching its head. A squeak sliced the air, then Tehlor turned the brown-and-white body upside down and slicked her palm with the blood pouring from its severed neck. Tiny hands twitched, and the furry thing seized, clutched in her clean fingers. Once her free hand was shiny and red, she dragged her palm from her forehead, over her nose and lips, and streaked her throat.

Bishop concealed a sob, whimpering softly. Their eyes bulged and they quaked all over, arms trembling, shoulders shaking. They shifted closer to Colin, pitching themself behind him.

"This is wrong," they whispered on a hitched breath. "Really, *really* fucking wrong—"

"To us, yes." He sighed through his nose. "Give her a moment."

"I can hear you," Tehlor said. She didn't bother looking at the two of them, just arranged her mason jars in a line and squeezed the lifeless rat above each one. Blood splattered the glass, spurting and coughing from the gaping area between its dainty shoulders. The rat's head sat upright on the cloth. Rectangular teeth poked over its bottom lip. Blood ringed the space around its ears. Once Tehlor had finished with the jars, she switched her attention to Colin and Bishop, grin severe and impish.

"Oh, c'mon. You've never bled a chicken, brujo?" She pointed at Bishop with the rat, then jabbed the body at Colin. "I *know* you've killed before, priest. It's a prerequisite in your religion."

"One, that's racist," Bishop snapped. "Two, get the hell out of my—"

"Tehlor, please," Colin said, flashing his hand in front of Bishop. "By the looks of how comfortable your rodent friend was when you arrived, I can only assume this isn't the first time it's faced your boline."

Bishop shot him a furious glance. "Her *what*?"

She heaved an exaggerated sigh and rolled her eyes, laying the rat's body on the cloth. She pinched the head between her fingers. Aligned the two separate pieces and leaned over the bloody mess, sending a glob of saliva onto the red seam where spine met skull. Bishop grunted their displeasure and turned into Colin, hiding their face against his arm. He wanted to tell them to watch, wanted them to see what magic could do when it was bargained for, paid for, earned by way of brutality, but he squeezed their knuckles instead. Held his breath and waited for the rat to shudder and stir, re-entering life in a violent spasm.

"It's her familiar," Colin explained, speaking lowly. He nudged Bishop with his shoulder and nodded toward the gore in the foyer.

Bishop lifted their face. They'd gone a bit ashy, but they relaxed at the sight of the rat, sitting on its haunches, cleaning its face with tiny paws.

"Thank you, Gunnhild," Tehlor said. She opened her hand, inviting the rat into her palm. Gunnhild scurried along Tehlor's sleeve and took her place on the witch's shoulder. Tehlor's face was a shock against the rest of the house, smeared red and still smiling. She pushed the jars a few inches apart with her feet, arranging them to her liking behind the couch, and then flipped her hands palm up.

The house pulled inward, as if the baseboards tried to detach from the walls, and the staircase attempted to unbuckle from the floor. Air stirred and shifted, carrying a litany of whispers and moans. The temperature plummeted. Slowly, creatures materialized, hugging the ceiling, crawling beneath the window, clutching the banister. Bishop flattened their palm on their chest and inhaled sharply. They caught themself on the doorframe, heaving through painful breaths. Their pupils slitted and a flush darkened their face, energy pulsing from them in strong waves.

"Like calls to like," Colin said. He rolled his sleeves to his elbows, displaying the raised edges on his runic tattoos. "She's performing an—"

"Uncloaking spell," Tehlor said. Light gathered in her palm, as if the sun had struck a faceted mirror. Blinding shards bounced around the house. "Can't find the dust bunnies unless we're able to see them—ah, there you are." She cooed at the ghoul on the ceiling. It chittered excitedly, face contorted by a bone-like beak. The inhuman horror gripped the ceiling with long, crooked hands. Two smoldering shards erupted from its back, raining soot and belching smoke.

Colin pressed his thumb against the crucifix at the end of his rosary. *Lesser demon*, he thought. *Rejected by God and man, given safe harbor by the fallen*. An apology sparked and died on his tongue.

Tehlor spun the ethereal light blooming in her palm. She hummed through confident laughter and struck her hands together. The sound cracked like thunder. Light speared the room. Bishop flinched. Colin did too. But it was the demon who fell, shaken loose from its perch and sent crashing to the floor.

"Hello, little beast," Tehlor whispered. She crouched, staring at the birdlike creature. Her pupils had expanded into twin black suns. "Be joyful, for you will feed a great serpent, and your bones will sit beneath the thrones of the Æsir."

The demon screeched, writhing on the floor. The light—whatever she'd conjured—had paralyzed it. She plunged her blade between the stumps on its back. The creature didn't bleed, it simply peeled away, disintegrating into grayish ash, and was seized by the thick, cold blood crawling along the side of an overturned mason jar. The blood moved as if alive, pulling the demon's shredded body into the jar with it, squirming and constricting, masticating and throbbing.

"Jesus . . ." Bishop whispered.

"We all make our deals," Colin said, watching Tehlor screw a lid over the jar. "We all pay our prices."

Their throat worked around a swallow. "Yeah, I know."

The next three spirits were more difficult to wrangle. Tehlor taunted a shadow into the light concealed in her closed fist, squeezing the stolen life from it once it slinked into her space. A ghoulish beast skittered across the floor, skin charred, razor-edge bone pushing through the places elbows, knees, vertebrae should've been, and snapped its square teeth when she jammed her knife through the bottom of its chin. Colin recited prayers to himself. Listened to shrieks and howls. He exhaled a sigh of relief when she sealed the last jar shut.

"Well, aren't you two cute," Tehlor purred, swatting nonexistent dust from her palms. She glanced at Bishop's fingers linked through Colin's knuckles.

Bishop stepped away, detaching from him, and picked their fallen McMuffin up off the floor, dropping it into the paper bag. "Are you done?"

"That didn't sound like 'thank you for saving my ass, Tehlor Nilsen', but I guess I can . . ." Her voice faded. Jaw slackened. All at once, the house clenched, tensing like a strained ligament, and she whipped toward the hallway. A sound echoed—the basement door creaking open—and dress shoes clicked the floor. "My, my, my," she whispered, darting her tongue across her top lip. "And who might you be?"

The hair on Colin's neck stood. He jolted forward, but Bishop caught his arm and stepped in front of him, loping across the room. They slid to a stop, shielding Tehlor with an outstretched arm.

"Lincoln, don't," they warned.

Tehlor glanced at their arm, then lifted her chin, granting Lincoln a curious once-over.

Lincoln stood in a crisp white shirt and tailored black pants. His charcoal jacket appeared freshly ironed, fixed with polished buttons, and his smooth black collar ringed the place where fur met flesh. Amber eyes glinted in the mid-morning sunlight pouring through the window. His wet nose twitched, and his pointed ears angled briefly toward Colin, tracking tentative movement near the couch.

"You let the exorcist bring a heretic into our home," Lincoln said. He lifted his maw, sniffing the air in front of Tehlor. "A cowardly, weak-willed Völva."

"Says the man half-made in the image of the true gods," Tehlor hissed, craning toward Lincoln. "You walk in Fenrir's shadow, demon pet. Be glad."

Bishop shoved her backward. "Enough," they snapped, and flashed their palm in front of Lincoln. "I brought her here—me, no one else."

Colin wound the rosary around his knuckles, smoothing his thumb along the crucifix. This had been a risk—he'd known that, so had Bishop—but he hadn't prepared for what might happen if Tehlor directly challenged Marchosias. *Witches*, he thought, *always cocky*.

Dried blood flaked on her coarse brows. She narrowed her eyes, baring her teeth in a sarcastic grin, held at bay by Bishop's locked elbow.

"A trinity of betrayals, then," Lincoln said. Smoke leaked from his mouth, and heat billowed outward, rising from the floor beneath him. His hellish muzzle crinkled into a snarl.

Before Colin could lunge forward, Bishop pressed their palm to Lincoln's chest. "Don't," they tested, retracting their outstretched arm and planting their free hand on his throat. "Lincoln, please." They spoke intimately, hushed words designed for midnight stirrings. "*Don't.*"

Colin sidestepped Lincoln and Bishop. He bumped Tehlor as he reached backward and twisted the doorknob.

"Go," he whispered, staring intently at shared touches: Bishop brushing their knuckles across Lincoln's narrow jawline, Lincoln catching Bishop's chin with his thumb. Colin glanced over his shoulder. "We can handle this."

"They have my number. Text me; I'll bring a bigger jar next time," Tehlor teased. She backed out of the house, cradling the rat, Gunnhild, in her palm and carrying souls in her farmers' market basket. Her eyes were still pinned to Lincoln. "Good luck. I hope your god listens."

"Me too." Colin gave a curt nod, eased the door shut, and twisted the heavy lock. He didn't know whether to haul Bishop back by their sleeve or stand at the ready, snared in iron-fisted jealousy. Truthfully, the latter was his only option.

Sulfur still hung in the air and smoke curled toward the ceiling, leaking from Lincoln's nostrils, and sliding between his elongated teeth. He tipped his face toward Bishop, leaned into their tentative touches, hands climbing his chest, fingertips dusting the curved space behind his lupine ears, and met Colin's stony gaze over Bishop's shoulder.

Strange, how actions once sewn with love could stop a monster in its tracks.

Lincoln trailed his hand underneath Bishop's sweater, touching the sensual dip on their lower back.

"A quartet of betrayals," Bishop said. Regret filled their eyes, soaked their voice. They gripped Lincoln's face; hands buried in the fur stretched over his wolf-shaped skull. Gold dripped from one side of their straight nose and slid over their shaky lips. "De las tinieblas vienes, de las tinieblas te vas."

Recognition sparked. Lincoln tried to rip himself away, but Bishop's magic had already coiled around his kneecaps. Gold vines gripped his legs and dragged him backward. He made a terrible noise, a guttural enraged growl, and snapped his teeth at Bishop's face. Bishop didn't flinch. They averted their eyes, though. Stared helplessly at the ground, repeating the spell until Lincoln was gone, leaving a sorrowful yelp rippling toward the vaulted ceiling.

Again, the house refused to breathe.

Colin stared at Bishop's flexed shoulders. Startled when they wiped their nose, wetting their knuckles with gilded blood. He cleared his throat.

"You bleed when you cast?" he asked.

They sniffled, mouth still reddened and glinting like a jewel. "Deals and prices, right?"

He nodded slowly. "Yes, I suppose that's the case with everything. Are you okay?"

"Tired," they said through a sigh. They hung their head back and closed their eyes, touching the tip of each finger to their thumb. Muted light graced the length of their throat. "We probably can't rob the cemetery during the day."

"We *could*, but we certainly shouldn't."

Bishop cracked their eyes open. "I bought us a few hours. Maybe we should get some sleep."

"Here?"

"Where else? You're the one that insisted Tehlor—who turned out to be a legitimate psychopath, by the way—would be an energy-efficient way to handle this shit. We'll need to be rested and alert for the Lazarus trial, practice, ritual—"

"Effect."

"*Whatever*. If your necro-technique doesn't kick our ass, my ex will," they said, exasperated. "So let's sleep while we can, all right? Get the fire goin'; I'll grab blankets."

Despite the worry festering in his depths, Colin did as he was told. He piled logs in the fireplace and lit them with a candlelighter, cinched the gauzy curtains in front of the window and chided his runaway heart.

I should be preparing. He stretched across the quilt Bishop had thrown down between the brick hearth and the coffee table. *I should be convening with the Holy Spirit.*

Bishop took off their glasses and laid beside him, nuzzling their face into a throw pillow. Their lashes cast shadows along their cheeks. Firelight licked their face, deepening the dark circles beneath their eyes. Colin imagined snaking his arm around their waist, but he refrained.

"Why didn't you come to my room last night?" Bishop asked. Hushed. Accidental, almost.

Colin thumbed crusted blood off their chin. A knot formed in his throat—twisted low in his belly.

"Because you terrify me," he said, and it was the truth.

Bishop hiccupped on a quiet laugh and closed their eyes.

Colin studied their plush, pink mouth. He didn't remember falling asleep.

CHAPTER NINE

MIST SLITHERED BETWEEN HEADSTONES AND frost clung to wilted bouquets at the Gold Hill cemetery, settled in an abandoned lot behind a recently demolished trailer park. Far enough from the road to conceal their efforts; close enough to send the pair skittering toward the ground whenever distant headlights crossed the trees.

Colin smacked the bottom of his shoe against a rusted shovel, scooping thawed dirt into the metal mouth. Hours ago, he'd woken on the living room floor with Bishop tucked beneath his chin. Their breath had warmed the ugly, hand-shaped scab on his throat, while his fingers sought their skin as they slept, slipping along their spine to settle over their neatly clasped bra. Colin had stayed awake, quietly breathing, devouring an intimate mishap. When Bishop had stirred, he'd pretended to be asleep again. Felt their fingers on his cheek and heard the floor wheeze as they'd tiptoed to the bathroom.

The two of them had dressed separately. Colin gathered supplies, Bishop fixed sandwiches, and neither of them talked about Tehlor's spirit jars, or Lincoln's presence, or the dreamless nap they'd shared by the fireplace.

Under a waxing gibbous moon, Colin turned graveyard earth while Bishop stole heat from a candle and used their magic to defrost the ground.

"I realize I've never asked," he said, tossing another pile of cold dirt over his shoulder. "How did . . . I mean." He paused, considering his next words carefully. "What did Lincoln's autopsy report say?"

"How'd I get away with it," Bishop said. They framed the question as a statement and their tired sigh fogged the air. "I used one spell to unstitch a valve in his heart, another to close the wound. Made it look like an aortic aneurysm."

Smart. "I see."

They pulled their wool coat tighter and adjusted the thick beanie covering their shorn hair. Switched a flickering candle from one hand to the other, encased in cylindrical glass wrapped in a vibrant rendition of the Blessed Mother. After another bout of warmth sank into the grave-pit, Bishop set the candle atop the headstone. *Lincoln Stone—Cherished Husband, Respected Veteran, Eternally Missed.* They tossed the second shovel into the hole and hopped inside.

Colin wiped his brow. "I understand you've probably prepared for this, but he *will* be a corpse."

"*Will he?*" Bishop mock-gasped, propping their arms on the handle of the shovel.

"Yes, it could be quite alarming."

"I appreciate the sentiment, but I'll be fine. It's not like you've exhumed many bodies either. I mean, I'm pretty sure there's a religious law about grave robbing, isn't there?"

"Federal law, yes. Religious law . . ." Colin waggled his hand back and forth. "The Catholic Church has absolutely put a corpse on trial before. Eight ninety-seven, the Vatican versus Pope Formosus. The court dressed him in holy robes, propped him in a chair, and accused him of perjury." He pushed his hair off his forehead. "And no—I haven't exhumed many bodies, but I *am* Catholic."

"So this isn't your first time?"

"Third or fourth, I believe."

Bishop snorted. "Comforting."

The two of them continued digging, panting hard, lifting heavy piles, slamming metal through the dirt. Evening air cooled the sweat beading on Colin's face, and Bishop stopped to unfasten the silver clasps on their coat.

Finally, a loud *thump* filled the pit. Colin's shovel connected with the casket and sent tremors rattling through his arms. He scraped the residual dirt away and pointed to the hunting tarp folded in the corner of the grave-pit. "Are you ready?"

Bishop leaned their shovel against the dirt wall. "I have to be."

There was a way to package desperation like this. The kind early in healing, late in making. But Colin had never been one to compartmentalize his pain. In his own desperation, he'd found himself tearing at the edges of a bandaged box, unable to rectify his loss with Isabelle's freedom. She hadn't left him, yet he'd lost her. Watching Bishop in his peripheral, he recognized the same uncaged feeling: a wounded animal reluctant to be contained. Yes, there was a way to package desperation, but Bishop Martínez was not the type to shelve their sorrow or bury their grief or smother their anger, and even though he'd found a way past his own trauma, Colin understood why Bishop stared at Lincoln's mahogany casket, why they refused to look away.

Colin waited for Bishop to unfasten the metal bracket attached to the casket's lid, and then curled his fingers around the wooden edge. He glanced at Bishop, waiting for *stop* or *don't*, but they didn't make a sound. Their chest stilled. They planted their hands next to Colin's and shoved the lid upward.

Dirty hinges snapped apart, loose earth fell onto his shoes, and sulfurous rot permeated the pit. Lichen grew in thatches along the left side of Lincoln's face. Teal moss webbed in his eyebrow, but the embalming fluid deposited into his carotid and midsection had kept his body intact. Besides his blotchy, ashen complexion and straw-like hair, Lincoln was the same man he'd been in the Polaroid. Square-jawed, knife-sharp, and deadly handsome.

Bishop inhaled shakily. "I thought he'd look worse."

"Formaldehyde is a miracle worker," Colin said. He flattened the edge of the tarp with his shoe. "I can do this part alone, Bishop. I'll just need help lifting—"

"I'm . . . I'm fine," they said under their breath, then again, snappish and angry, "I'm *fine*."

Guilt withered in Colin's chest. He nodded. Dipped his hands underneath Lincoln's arms, ignoring the scratchy fabric of his service uniform, and tugged his stiffened body out of the casket. Bishop caught the corpse's pelvis, shuffled backward over the tarp, and dropped his legs. They blew out a breath and pursed their wobbling lips. Shook out their hands. Cracked their neck.

Lincoln Stone, ripened by death, human and empty, rolled lifelessly inside the olive tarp. Colin breathed easier once the tarp had been zip-tied around Lincoln's ankles and above his head. He pushed the lower half of the body while Bishop stood aboveground and hauled the bloated bundle onto flat ground. Bishop didn't speak, they hardly lifted their gaze, and Colin didn't know whether to reach for them or keep his distance. A part of him wanted to say *I understand*, but he didn't; another part of him wanted to say *it will get better*, but he knew it wouldn't. Grief, and betrayal, and fine-tuned desperation were learned, lived, and endured. People got better from a burst cyst, from an undercooked pork chop, from an impromptu breakup. But no one fully recovered from loss like this. They simply adapted to the sound of it, calloused to the feel of it.

Still, Colin wished he had the strength to lie to them. Spit false hope at their feet and smile. But he honored their silence and helped them refill the grave-pit. Both shovels crunched through the snowy dirt. Pebbles and ice smacked the closed casket and echoed into the night, dulling as the pit gradually shallowed. Colin fixed the rectangular mound cover back into place, blanketing Lincoln's grave with loose grass, and stopped to catch his breath, watching Bishop clip the extra waterproof tarp over the bed of their truck.

There, he thought. *The easy part is done.*

He swatted dirt off his hands and climbed into the passenger seat. Bishop shut the driver's-side door. They held the still-burning votive in both hands and inhaled, sucking the flame between their lips. Their throat glowed, as did their eyes and the seam of their mouth. When they exhaled, steam billowed into the cab, folding against the chilled windshield. *What a beautiful thing,* Colin thought. *Taking in, letting go.* He rested his cheek on the headrest and watched their swirling, flame-tinged breath dissipate.

"Are you still fine?" Colin tested.

Bishop fiddled with their keys, staring through the windshield.

"I don't know," they said, and it sounded like the truth.

The moon's white smile hardly lit the sky and the slim sidewalk lamps skewering the trees only partially illuminated the cemetery, leaving grave sites and mausoleums bathed in darkness. In the distance, the on-site chapel glowed, flecked with memory candles and stationed by a lazy security guard. Everything else succumbed to the night. The two of them shared the silence together, flushed from exertion, sweat-dampened and carrying dust on their clothes.

"Do I really terrify you?" Bishop asked, their voice a weak thing in the confined space.

"Yes." It was an easy truth to tell.

They furrowed their brows and let their lips peel apart, expression falling from confusion to abrupt sadness. "*Why . . . ?*"

Colin inhaled deeply and sighed through his nose. "Because you're extraordinary," he said, and turned toward the passenger window. There was no use lying to them. No use attempting to dilute how he felt or skirt the edge of his intrigue. "I tend to appreciate distance, but somehow, I haven't found the fortitude to stop wanting you. I think about you often: when I'm awake, when I'm asleep, when I'm alone. Do you know what that's like?" He huffed out an annoyed breath and glanced at Bishop, blushing hot. "To find yourself trapped in an unexpected orbit? To know someone's power, to understand their pain, to get a glimpse of their heart?" He met their wide, tense eyes. "Before I slept with you, I daydreamed about you. Now that I've been with you, I'm consumed by you. How I feel about you, what I want from you . . . it's thrilling; it's excruciating. So, yes, you terrify me, Bishop."

Bishop stayed exceedingly still. They stared, expression unreadable, and let the silence grow.

I'm a damn fool, Colin thought. His pulse quickened and he shifted his gaze to the window again. *Stupid, childish idiot—*

The prayer candle landed in the cup holder, and Bishop surged across the middle seat. They gripped Colin's cheek and turned his face toward them, seizing his mouth in a firm kiss. Colin remembered to breathe as he pawed at their waist, clumsy and eager in the cramped cab. For a moment, he couldn't recall a damn thing he'd said. Only *daydreamed*, only *consumed*, only *terrify*. The truth ached in his chest. How badly he'd craved them, how his desire for them had suffocated his lonely heart. Wanting and being wanted had been unimaginable, yet Bishop was there, crawling into his lap, sliding their thighs around his waist. They were there, prying at his lips, mouth still candle-hot and tinged with magic. *There*, surrounding him, holding on to him.

"Be scared of me," they rasped, breathing hard against his chin. "But don't be afraid to touch me."

Colin palmed their denim-clad thighs, eased along the crease of their hips, and hauled them closer. Each kiss slowed and stretched, widening for damp, hot breath, and soft, warm tongues. Bishop moaned, a rough sound that curled intimately around Colin's bones. They inched their fingers into his hair, pressed their thumbs into his temples, clutched his face and angled him where they wanted—closer, upward, into them. They touched the place where their lips met and sent a gusting breath into Colin's depths. Magic pulsed inside him, fluttering restlessly, flavored like Bishop, like raw, holy power, like everything he'd left behind.

Colin eased away, detaching from the dizzying energy riding the back of Bishop's breath. Bishop nosed at his cheek, tried to tug him into another kiss, but he ducked under their chin and set his teeth around their heartbeat, working a bruise onto their skin. They cradled the back of his skull. Sucked in shaky breath. Rolled sensually in his lap, pressing the taut fabric between their thighs against his hip bone. Colin felt their magic sting beneath his tattoos, settling in the arcs and grooves of mystic runes and angel-speak. Power recognized power. Like called unceremoniously to like.

Lincoln Stone's corpse was strewn in the bed of the truck, wrapped and contained, hollow and silent, waiting to be occupied. Colin couldn't fathom leaving the cemetery, though. Couldn't bear to take his hands off Bishop, couldn't stand the idea of being anywhere else.

Marchosias be damned, he would touch them until they babbled and begged, he would kiss them until their mouth knew nothing but the shape of his lips, he would hold them until they said *let me go*, and God, he hoped and prayed that those three words never surfaced.

When he fumbled with the button on their jeans, their spine bent and their chest stuttered, and when he slid his fingers into their mouth, they took his digits willingly, eyes half-lidded, cheeks blazing, sucking wetly on his knuckles. They were astonishingly beautiful. Carnal and haughty and undone.

"Look at me," he said, and worked his hand between their legs.

Bishop did as they were told. They loosened their jaw and stared at Colin, reaching for his palm in jilting pulses. He wanted to touch them reverently, to worship at the altar of their hips and watch moonlight skate across their body, but they were crowded against him in a humid truck with their shirt bunched above their belly button, and he wasn't about to complain. They strained against unforgiving denim and attempted to spread their legs, sighing contentedly as Colin pushed his fingers inside them. The night carried remnants of what they'd done. Broken frozen ground, turned soil and shoveled dirt, exhumed the body of someone Bishop had once loved—still loved. Despite their hunger, he tasted anguish on their lips, sorrow in the kisses they stole, and tried to slow, to gentle, to treat them tenderly.

"Don't," they snapped, breathlessly. Bishop kissed him hard. Took his bottom lip between their teeth and bit. "C'mon, please. *Please.*"

Colin knew what it was like to find safety in pain. He understood the narrow space people searched for when they needed to be hurt and held and outside themselves. And even if he wanted something different, something intimate and visceral, this was real enough. Deep enough. Even if he wanted to be more for Bishop, he would be an escape for them. Tonight, at least. *Tonight.*

Evening deepened, and the windshield fogged, and Colin touched them until they were whining and gasping, sank his teeth into their supple skin until they said his name and bucked against him, kept his hand between their quivering thighs until their cunt clenched and spasmed. He gave them what they wanted: pain and pleasure, obedience and release.

But he hopelessly, selfishly wanted more.

Chapter Ten

"You warded this room, right?" Bishop asked. They braced their palms on their thighs and caught their breath, glancing from the basement staircase to where they'd propped Lincoln's stiff corpse in the awful floral recliner.

Colin nodded. He gestured loosely to a paper clipping perched on the banister, then another atop the washer, and another on stacked sheets stuffed in the linen shelf. Last night, when Colin had waded through bouts of lucidity, he'd sketched quarter-sized images of Saint Christopher, Michael the Archangel, and Saint Benedict in his notebook, flicked Holy Water onto the paper, then tore them from the page individually. The adapted Esszettel, faith-filled spells that typically chased ailments away, were charged with borrowed power. They acted like an invisibility cloak, filling the basement with protective energy. He swept his gaze from Bishop's dusty boots to their crooked glasses. An hour ago, the cemetery had been a safe haven, their breath on his throat, convincing his mangled skin to finish healing, their hand crammed inside his jeans, their lips on his jaw, cheek, temple, but it'd ended, as all things end, and Bishop had driven back to the house on Staghorn Way.

"Once we begin, there will be no going back," Colin said. He turned his attention to Lincoln, upright and rigid in the chair. Dirt clung to his dark hair and his eyelids had peeled apart, loosened by a cotton ball soaked in isopropyl alcohol. "And I can't guarantee swiftness. We could be done by sunrise. We could be done sometime next week. Next month, even. These things are unpredictable."

Bishop righted themself. "I texted Tehlor. Asked her to stop by if we don't touch base with her in a few hours."

"Ah, lovely."

"She told me I'd owe her if she had to save our asses."

"Of course."

"Better safe than sorry," they said, shrugging.

"I don't think she's exactly *safe*, but . . ." He shrugged too. "It's not a bad idea to have reinforcements on standby."

The house trembled. Baseboards flexed and the ceiling creaked, rippling beneath brutal footsteps. Walls bowed inward, doors rattled in their frames, the staircase wheezed, windowsills squeezed glass, and Marchosias sent a fearsome snarl reverberating through the air. Colin tipped his head, tracking the heavy movement on the ground floor. The Esszettel protected the basement, yes, but the wards had been inevitably noticed. Lincoln and Marchosias had become aware that a portion of the house was shut off from their eyes, and Bishop and Colin were out of time.

Colin said, "Light the candles."

Bishop knuckled their glasses into place, dug a lighter out of their pocket, and snatched the spark from where it jumped on the flint. The fire swayed in their palm, suspended above their heart line, and flickered as they lowered the flame toward each naked wick. The pillar candles cast white circles on the floor, stretched the shadows, deepened the hollow underground. Another growl shook the house. Colin looped rope around Lincoln's wrists and ankles. Muttered a prayer under his breath—*give me strength, Lord. Work through me*—then crossed the room where he plucked the coin-sized paper from inside the linen shelf. He studied the rendition of Michael and let his tainted blood call for the angel, sing praises of the High Court, reach and reach and *reach*. He closed his eyes, placed the paper on his tongue, and felt new energy needle his veins as he swallowed.

He glanced at Bishop as he made his way to the washer, chewed the image of Saint Christopher, and lifted a brow. "What?" he asked.

"You're eating paper, Colin. Don't *what* me."

"I assumed a witch, above anyone else, would understand the components of a spell."

"Is that what you're doing, casting a spell?"

"Asking for assistance," he said, biting out each word. "Don't look at me like I'm speaking in tongues."

Bishop rolled their eyes. "Can you explain, then?"

"I blessed these specific warding tools with holy iconography. They're used for protection, right?" He lifted his gaze and met Bishop's eyes. When they nodded, he continued. "So once they're removed from the space they've been tasked to protect, they'll shift their power somewhere else." He lifted the last Esszettel, Saint Benedict of Nursia, protector of exorcists, miracle worker blessed by God, and brought it to his mouth.

"Into you," Bishop said under their breath.

The house rocked through another shudder.

Colin sighed through his nose. "Brace yourself," he said, and sucked the paper between his molars. "He'll return as the man you remember and like nothing you've ever encountered before. Once we transfer his incorporeal form into the vessel, Marchosias and Lincoln will try their best, separately and together, to break you down, to get inside your head—inside your heart—and rip you apart. Do you understand?"

Bishop searched his face. Their jaw flexed, shoulders pulled taut, fingers curling and uncurling at their sides. "I get it, yeah."

"Good," Colin said. He thought about kissing them, but he stared instead. Remembered their smile pressed against his cheek, their body curled against his chest by the fireplace, and he *hoped*.

The last Esszettel made its way down his throat, and pure, ethereal light leaked like oil into every limb, coated every bone, hummed in every tooth. He sucked in a sudden, fearful breath and watched Bishop take a step backward. His eyes reflected like quartz in the lenses on their glasses, glowing ghostly white, and his name coasted from them on an uncertain breath. They bumped the staircase, catching themself on the banister.

Be with me, he thought. He rolled his sleeves to his elbows. Black ink raised like fresh scars on his skin. *Stay with me.*

There wasn't much time between the angelic power taking root inside Colin and the sound of footsteps on the stairs. Shoes, first. Then too many paws. Rushing wind inside a closed-up house.

Lincoln arrived in starts and stops. He was on the stairs, straight-spined and regal, and then he shifted to all fours, snarling with his ears pinned. His image jolted backward, forward, backward again, until he managed to step into the basement and right himself against the animal, demon, *beast* tethered to his soul. Colin had no time to adjust. One moment, he was struggling to breathe through the influx of *holy* and *yes* and *ancient* pulsing inside him, and the next, Lincoln had whipped toward his stationary corpse, eyes wide, muzzle curled into a wet snarl.

"What is this, priest?" Lincoln spat. He turned and snapped his teeth at Bishop. His eyes cracked, softening in the flickering candlelight. "What've you let him do to me?"

Bishop parted their lips and clutched the banister, flattened with their back against the wall attached to the staircase. They shook their head. "Don't act like this is betrayal, Lincoln. This is . . . This is *reaction*. These are consequences."

"Bishop," Colin warned. He inched forward, ready to snatch Lincoln by the collar.

They continued. "You groomed me, you tricked me, and you stole from me. My blood, my essence, my . . . my fucking *power* wasn't yours to take. *I* wasn't yours to use."

"We took vows," Lincoln said. The timbre in his voice vibrated the basement, human and not, heartbroken and not. "You swore to love me, to stand beside me—"

"Until you died," Bishop hollered. Lincoln flinched as if he'd been struck. They set their jaw, expression hard despite the tremor in their chin. When they spoke, each word gusted from them, painfully, slowly. "And now here we are."

The quiet unraveled. Lincoln stared at Bishop, canine eyes narrowed, ears perked, muzzle set calmly. When he reached for them, Colin bristled, but Bishop didn't wince or step away. They allowed Lincoln to touch their jaw, to dust his knuckles across their cheek, the same place he'd struck them days ago, and they made a tiny, broken sound when he curled his fingers around their throat—squeezing. His thumb found the bruise Colin's mouth had left behind. They gripped his wrists and wobbled on their tiptoes, inhaling sharply through their nose.

"*Love . . . ?*" they wheezed. Their pupils slitted. Magic pulsed through their skin, sending gilded light bouncing around the basement. "Is this love?"

"Is that?" Lincoln asked. He nudged his maw toward the corpse in the recliner.

Dread opened like a pit in Colin's stomach. He reached for the light writhing beneath his skin and brought his palms together, sending a crisp *gong* reverberating around the room. The sound mimicked a church bell, metallic and deep, and caused Lincoln to retract his hand and slap his palms over his folded ears. Lincoln curled inward, spine arching, bone splintering, becoming more animal, more demon, until the sound faded and Marchosias paused his assault on their conjoined form. Lincoln opened his jaw for a fierce snarl. His elongated, slickened teeth shone pearl white, sprouting from pink gums. His shoulders hunched defensively, and he bent his knuckles, sending horrid, howling noise toward Colin.

"By God, I have provided safe harbor," Colin said, projecting over the growl bubbling in Lincoln's throat. "I have brought to you, by grace and humility, a vessel for your lost soul, a place for the damned to reside, and I command thee—demon, wretched, unclean—to cross into this abandoned body." He looped his rosary around his palm, settling his thumb over the cross dangling from the bottom bead, and pressed the crucifix to the corpse's cold forehead. "Like our friend Lazarus, you have fallen into dreadful sleep, and I have come to wake you."

Lincoln stormed forward. He pitched his body toward Colin, but Bishop intercepted, sending a golden rope around their ex-husband's ankle. The light came from nowhere and everywhere, shooting through the floor like vines, falling through the ceiling to catch on

Lincoln's belt. Bishop kept their hand outstretched, shaking with exertion, holding Lincoln at bay.

"I call upon the resurrectionist, sanctifier of life, take this soul and give him breath," Colin shouted. He shifted his gaze to Bishop and gave a curt nod.

All at once the light blinked out, the ethereal ropes vanished, and Lincoln bounded forward. Teeth grazed his hand, slicing pale skin, but Colin met his mark and grasped Lincoln's face in a confident grip.

"Like Lazarus, I wake thee," he shouted. Lincoln thrashed, but his movements turned choppy and malformed. "Like Lazarus, I wake thee!"

Across the room, Bishop sniffled. A few candles winked and dimmed, simmering out one by one. Loamy wind cracked through the basement, tossing smoke from smoldering wicks, rustling Bishop's clothes, gusting along Colin's rosary, and made for the corpse. Colin felt the transference like electricity. Lincoln and Marchosias shocked through his body, rattled his skeleton, and began to disintegrate.

Beneath his palm, Lincoln's wolfish head peeled away. Became ash and soot. Floated into the strange, mud-scented airstream and rushed into the body tied to the recliner. Shot into the corpse's nostrils, filled Lincoln's empty ear canals, dry eye sockets, and snaked past his chapped lips. Like a swarm of locusts, Lincoln and Marchosias filled Lincoln's bloodless corpse, and on a painful, sandy cough, the dead reanimated.

"Like Lazarus, let it be done," Colin spat, panting. He lowered his hand from where it'd hovered in midair and pushed the crucifix into Lincoln's waxy flesh. "Like Lazarus, you are reborn."

Lincoln opened his eyes. He immediately jerked against the restraints, hissing through his teeth once the rope snared his skin. Colin stepped away and straightened in place. He brushed invisible dust from his sweater and cracked his neck, granting Lincoln a proper once-over.

Lincoln Stone carried the same primal, caged look Isabelle had before she died. The same expression Bishop had worn in the cemetery. Flighty gaze, dilated pupils, bared teeth. *Desperation*, he thought, *a wounded animal reluctant to be contained.* He searched Lincoln's eyes, colored like Paraiba tourmaline, and snorted dismissively. The divinity thrumming in his runic tattoos made him brave or stupid. Both, perhaps.

"Priest," Lincoln said. He spat at Colin's tightly laced shoes. "I told you, didn't I? Their heart is a bear trap."

"I'm not a priest, and their heart is none of my business," Colin said. He curled his knuckles inward, flexing his fists.

"Ah, but you've made it your business. Or are you only interested in their juicy—"

Colin struck Lincoln with the back of his hand. The connection, hard knuckles against sallow cheek, clapped through the dimly lit room. Bishop inhaled raggedly, as if they had something to say, but opted for silence instead. Colin glanced at them. Met their eyes for a heartbeat, then two, before he shifted his attention back to Lincoln.

"Like I said, I'm no priest," he rasped, assessing reddened knuckles. "Technically, I'm hardly an exorcist anymore. Specialist is more appropriate. Would you like to know what I specialize in?"

Lincoln licked dark, tar-like blood—embalming fluid and distressed flesh—from his split lip. "No," he drawled, and hissed something in a dead language. Latin, maybe. Or Aramaic. "You bore me, churchling. I've heard better stories from liquor-poached sailors and New York vagrants."

Colin pulled leather gloves from his back pocket and fingered them into place over each hand. "I extract beings like you from dwellings like this. I do so gently, as often as I can, but I take no issue in severing you from this place by force if you refuse to leave willingly. Do you understand, Marchosias?"

An awful, choked-off noise left Lincoln's mouth. Low, like a wolf chomping bone. He parted his lips, but his face remained unmoving. An eerie, familiar sound tumbled off his stationary tongue.

"Do you understand, Marchosias?" Lincoln parroted, but it was Isabelle in the room. Her honeyed voice landed like a wasp on Colin's ear. The corpse flashed yellowing teeth, gums caked in blackened blood, and hiccupped through cruel laughter. "You're famous, Colin Hart," Lincoln said, returning to his rich, venomous voice. "So far from God, so close to Hell, so rich in sin. More like us than you think, yes?"

"Enough," Bishop barked.

"And you, mighty brujo," Lincoln seethed, craning toward them. "Such power and no sense to use it. What a waste . . ." He paused, brow furrowing, mouth squirming, as if two halves of a whole warred within him. He settled for an indignant snort and flicked his eyes to Colin. "Aren't they magnificent? Entirely *raw*," he whispered, widening his mouth for the word. "Still becoming, still searching for someone to unleash their potential. How 'bout you, exorcist? Will you jam yourself inside them again? Pick all their locks? Or will you put a knife to their throat?"

Colin brushed past Bishop and crossed the room, retrieving a white bottle from atop the washer. He twisted the lid, dumped Holy Water into his palm, and flicked droplets onto Lincoln's bare skin. Smoke ribboned away from the singe marks dotting the tops of Lincoln's hands and the bridge of his sloped nose. He writhed in his restraints. Bowed away from the recliner and flared his nostrils, bared his teeth, and kicked at the concrete floor.

Stay steady, Colin thought. Isabelle's saccharine voice had unnerved him. He could hardly concentrate without hearing an echo of her behind every thought.

"I adjure thee, demon," Colin said, leveling his tone, and rained blessed water on Lincoln again. "You are cast out—exit this body, this place, this dwelling."

When Lincoln Stone peeled his eyes open, he blinked at Bishop. Gasped and shuddered and breathed like a frightened deer. "Bishop," he whispered, straining against rope and divinity. "Baby, please. I'm in . . . I'm in pain, okay? It's like someone's got ahold of my organs, like I'm bein' pulled apart." He heaved in another great breath. Like most exorcisms, Colin halfway believed him. Understood longing, recognized the regret vining around his vocal cords. "I didn't know it'd be like this. I—I didn't mean to . . . to hurt you. I'd never—you *know* that—you know I'd never—"

Colin arched an eyebrow. "Utilize their blood without permission? Torture them in the home you used to share? Smack them—"

"Watch your mouth, priest," Lincoln snapped, growled and shouted, howled and snarled. Man and not, human and not. He leaned as far forward as he could, jutting his face toward Bishop. "I haven't stopped loving you. Why do you think I'm still here, huh? Why would I stay . . . ?"

Bishop stood with their hackles raised, swaying uncertainly on their feet. Gold glittered in the blood ringing their nostrils, and their throat moved around a slow swallow.

"Because you needed me," they said, so, *so* softly. Love, dead or alive, somewhere between the two, still clawed at them. Colin saw it in their glassy eyes, knew it in their loose shoulders and open, empty hands. Love, like possession, like a haunting, refused to rest.

"That's what he told you, right?" Lincoln said. "Before or after he fucked you? C'mon, Bishop. Think for a minute. Of course he told you that. He's tryin' to crawl back under the Vatican's wing and you're an easy way to make that happen."

Their mouth tightened.

"Don't listen to him," Colin tested, watching Bishop carefully.

Lincoln rambled. "He'll do anything to buy his way back in. *Anything!* You know that; you know—"

"I cut your heart in half," they said, hardly whispering, hardly speaking at all. Their voice wobbled, strained and callous. "And I know the only reason I'm alive is because you needed me to *stay* alive. You can't out-witch me, Lincoln, and you can't outsmart me, and you can't outmaneuver me. I'm what you wanted to become, remember?"

Gold flooded their sclera, sharpening their pupils into points. The remaining flame-tipped candles stretched their shadow into the shape of a jaguar on the wall behind them, lengthened by the banister, turned huge and monstrous by trapped light.

"I know who you are—I know who you *were*. And I . . ." They faltered, inhaling roughly through their nose. "I'm letting you go, Lincoln Stone. I'm banishing you from my body, I'm banishing you from my soul, I'm banishing you from this house . . ."

Lincoln snapped his blunt teeth at the air. "You think stabbing me made you strong?" He spat out a laugh. Holy water still singed his skin, opening like pink pools on broken flesh. Hunger rippled outward, darkening his voice, turning his eyes solid black. "*Please.* You were nothing but a kitchen witch before me, singing lullabies to bay leaves and carving wellness spells into corn husks."

"And look at me after you," Bishop said. Heat flooded the basement—desert heat, the sweltering kind that burned on every breath, made a person squint and recoil, caused lungs to shrink and squeeze.

Their shadow crawled along the wall, detaching from their ankles to creep around the back of the recliner.

Damn.

Colin stepped in front of Bishop. "Hey, look at me," he said, ducking to find their golden gaze. "Bishop—*hey*." They tore their eyes away from Lincoln and stared at Colin, lashes flicking, brow tense and wrinkled. Power pulsed from them. Rippled off their skin like wind skipping waves. "If you kill him again, it starts all over," he said as tenderly and truthfully as possible. "He exits the body, occupies the house, and we go back to square one. That's why he's pushing you. If you physically kill him or you spiritually kill him, he wins. Don't let him take this from you."

"Still trying to stifle you," Lincoln hollered. "Still trying to *save* you, because he couldn't save his sweet, soft-skinned Isabelle."

Bishop chewed their lip. Their feline shadow towered over Lincoln, jaws split for stormy teeth, paws flexed and blurred, looming in the air. "I'm taking back what's mine," they said. They tipped their chin toward Colin, roaming his face with quick, purposeful glances. Mouth, throat, eyes. "People don't get to *steal* without consequences. He doesn't get to colonize my fucking magic." They brushed his waist with their fingertips and stepped around him, slender digits undulating in quick, electric pulses. They swirled one hand through the air and their shadow reared back. "Don't worry—he'll live."

There was a frightening thrill to it: being in the same room as Bishop Martínez and their magic. Especially then, especially there, on the cusp of undoing their own haunting.

Bishop flicked their wrist and sent the catlike shadow into Lincoln's space, digging at his reanimated corpse with misty claws. Lincoln jerked away from the chair, gasping and shouting. The ropes left welts on his arms, Holy Water sizzled on his skin, and Colin almost flinched when Bishop's shadow wrenched open Lincoln's mouth and dug around inside him. Excavating. Yanking stolen magic from behind his teeth.

Bishop bent their fingers, knuckles whitening as Lincoln bucked and cried out. The house trembled. Beams creaked, the staircase wheezed, and windows vibrated, resisting the spiritual cut—the last, lingering attachment from Lincoln Stone to Bishop Martínez. Finally, the shadow found what it was searching for, and two golden flecks floated from the depths of Lincoln's throat.

The magic glinted, turning in the air like dust caught in a slow-motion breeze. Lincoln stared at the yellowish substance. His chest heaved, expression folding into defeat, and watched the magic cross the room, sinking delicately into Bishop's open palm.

Blood flowed in a thin rivulet from their left nostril, curving over their mouth, gathering on their chin and dripping onto their shirt. They breathed easier. Straightened in place and called their shadow back to them, swaying from exertion as the dark, translucent jaguar reattached to their ankles.

"Leave this place," Bishop said, sighing the words like a prayer.

Lincoln exhaled a hard, trembling breath. "Now, I can't protect you," he said, half-lidded eyes settled on Bishop. Colin heard the truth in his weak voice.

Bishop opened their mouth, but Colin stepped in front of them, guiding them backward with a gentle shove. He glanced over his shoulder and nodded curtly.

"You've done your part," he said, pushing one of his fallen sleeves to his elbow. Around them, wind stirred, and candles flickered. "Let me do mine."

"What . . ." They turned their gaze from Colin to Lincoln. Their pupils fanned outward, expanding, shrinking, and their slender throat flexed around a nervous swallow.

"I'm sorry," Lincoln whispered. He rested the back of his head against the recliner and closed his eyes. As two of the last three candles died, light became harder to find, shadows deepened, turned the atmosphere daunting and stagnant, and Colin readied himself for the inevitable.

Bones cracked, like a boot on a twig. Lincoln made a desperate, young noise—a muffled, choked-off cry—and his mouth shot open.

Colin patted Bishop's hip and said, "Stay behind me."

Like something out of a nightmare, long, clawed fingers curved around Lincoln's cheeks. Marchosias poured from his body in thick, black ropes, erupting in syrupy pulses. Oily substance crawled over Lincoln's face and throat, shaped like a breathing anemone, shifting like thorns on a liquid stem, and began to reshape itself.

Pointed ears, blocky muzzle, crimson eyes, leathery wings.

"Priest," Marchosias snarled. His voice was Lincoln, and Isabelle, and the echo of a thousand long-gone screams. He became great and terrible, swathed in midnight, baring his teeth in a wolfish grin. "You have been found wanting."

CHAPTER ELEVEN

COLIN HART HAD STUDIED DEMONOLOGY for many years, but he had never witnessed a possessor exit the possessed in the middle of an exorcism. He'd plunged into people like a train through a tunnel, he seeking light where darkness reigned. Reached between loose ribs and seized unsteady hearts. Shackled reckless spirits and removed the unwanted. But Marchosias, Marquis of Hell, would not go quietly. The demon prince kept hold of Lincoln, leaving his body half empty and gasping. The corpse appeared suddenly drawn, hollow-eyed and sunken, more dead than it had been when they'd pulled it from the grave.

"I want for nothing," Colin said, attempting to cool the heat in his voice. Power hummed in his runic tattoos, pressed on his sternum, and held fast to his bones.

"You're a liar, then," Marchosias said. His wings sprayed soot and ash, sending orange cinders bouncing too close to Colin's shoe. He stood on pawed feet, spine bent awkwardly at his mid-back, face harshly arranged. This close, he was difficult to see. Unearthly and inhuman. Completely and utterly unfathomable.

But Colin looked. He set his teeth and pushed his heels into the floor, forcing his body to balance against the churning in his stomach and the sulfur-tinged air. Even with an abomination before him, he would lift his chin and be brave. At that point, he had no other choice.

"I adjure thee, demon," Colin said, throwing the words like a fist. "Resume your place in the depths of Hell and let this home be free of you."

Laughter rumbled in Marchosias's throat, shaking the house. "You would be wise not to test me, Colin Hart. I was once an angel of domination myself—I know the law, I know the book—and you know, as well as I do, that I was called upon." A forked tongue licked over his black maw, and he tipped his head toward Lincoln. "Or are you willing to compromise a perfectly good soul in exchange for another notch on your belt?"

"Judgment isn't my job. Extraction is. Whatever the High Court has in store for Lincoln, they'll see it through," Colin said. He resisted the urge to take a step back. "There's nothing here for you, Marchosias."

Marchosias dragged his blood-colored eyes down Colin's body, then rested his gaze on Bishop. "Isn't there, though? Or is your power a lie?"

Colin channeled the searing light flooding through his veins. He felt Bishop inch closer, their hand brushing his palm, and stepped forward, flinging Holy Water at Marchosias. Flesh peeled and crackled on the demon's wolfish face, dotted open and sizzled on his concave chest.

Marchosias opened his mouth and sound cascaded out—thunder cracking, wolves howling, people wailing, eagles screeching. Smoke did too. Noxious black clouds swirled in the basement, causing Bishop to cough and choke. Colin squeezed his eyes shut, reached blindly, and prayed. *Find purchase in me*, he begged, gagging on toxic fumes. He found Bishop's elbow and grabbed them, stumbling backward. *Give me a weapon.*

"Resume my place in Hell?" Marchosias screamed, rising to stretch his wings toward the walls and swipe his claw through the air, catching Colin on the cheek. "There is no Hell, priest. No Heaven, no after, no cometh from. There is only here, the place we've been given, populated with your tiny, abandoned selves searching aimlessly for recognition, for sustenance, for our father's long-gone purpose. You were created out of nothing, destined to become *nothing*, and we—the fallen, the true heirs—are here to govern that nothingness—"

"Michael, protector, Saint in the Armory, deliver this soul as you see fit. Chain this terror and deliver us," Colin shouted. Pale light beamed from his palm and sliced through the smoke, sending plumes billowing upward and outward, reminiscent of the Red Sea. Colin sucked in a desperate breath. "Please," he said. A second time, weaker, "*please.*"

Don't abandon me again.

"Oh, to beg," Marchosias bellowed. "Do you taste riches, Colin Hart? Did you strike gold between your pretty nun's legs? Did your brujo drip like a peach when you suckled at the center of their universe? You cannot lie to me. Beg to whoever you think will listen, but know you are alone, know that I *witness* you. Steeped in sin. Left to rot, same as me."

Bishop clung to him. "Tell me what to do," they gasped out, pawing at Colin's chest, but he couldn't move, couldn't calm his panicked heart. The light shooting from his palm died. "*Colin!*"

Colin tried to gather a clean breath and choked. "Use your magic—shackle him if you can."

They reached for his face, shielding his eyes. Their hand slipped across his bloodied cheek, carved by Marchosias's black talon, and they stopped short. "Colin, you're—"

"Do it, Bishop! *Now!*"

Bishop flung their arm out. Gold spilled across the floor and latched around Marchosias's pawed feet. The wolf demon let out a horrifying howl, but Bishop's magic kept him in place for long enough to allow Colin time to breathe. To close his eyes and focus.

Do not leave me, he prayed. *Use me. Apprehend me. Allow me to be your vessel.* He called out to Michael, to Saint Benedict and Saint Christopher, to Raphael the healer, and Gabriel the honorable. *Be with me. Help me.*

Fire lit the basement. Orange flames seeded with black pits glowed on Marchosias's clawed fingertips.

Power came upon Colin in fistfuls. It almost knocked the wind from him. Almost buckled his knees, brought tears to his stinging eyes, caused the pain in his cheek to disappear. His body felt too big for him, suddenly. Too crowded with energy, skin bursting at the seams with *war*. He knew the cool sting of Michael's sword, heard the whisper of sainthood echo in his marrow, recognized the beat of Gabriel's wings against his heart, felt the stirring of Raphael on the soles of his feet, in the lines on his palms.

"Colin . . ." Bishop's hand loosened around his elbow.

"Don't be afraid," Colin said, but it was not him. Several voices lapped at each other, humming in the smoky air. He released his hold on his own bones, let go of his body and allowed himself to become a tool.

And so, his world drowned.

Colin felt four-fingered hands, pressing on his shoulders, brushing across his forehead, tugging at his skin. Heard a litany of angel-speak in the sunken place inside himself where his soul took shelter. Felt his limbs move, legs propelling his body forward, mouth forming words in a language he did not know. From behind his eyes, he saw the Marquis of Hell aim another blow at his face, but Colin caught the creature's hand.

I have you.

Shock flashed across Marchosias's crinkled muzzle. His eyes darted back and forth, taking in Colin Hart, who had surrendered to the High Court, who had been filled with divinity, and said, "Brother," like a curse. "How I have searched for you."

A sleek, heavy handle pressed against Colin's palm. He gripped the smooth leather, knew the weight of another hand resting atop his, and thrust the weapon forward. A blade forged from starlight punched through the demon's stomach—Michael's sword, a celestial reckoning—and time warped. Somewhere nearby, Bishop said his name, and somewhere distant, somewhere gone, Isabelle called to him. Marchosias surged, still speared on Michael's sword, and snatched Colin's face. The demon's oversized hand and extra knuckles gripped his jaw, fingers curving over his cheeks and digging into his temples.

"You will be hunted, Colin Hart," Marchosias spat.

Colin twisted the sword. Bone cracked and bent. A chorus of different voices lashed his lips. "You are guilty, Marchosias. Come and face your judgment."

Cosmic rope, shining white and silver, twined around Marchosias's throat, cuffed his ankles and wrists, and bound his wings. He thrashed against the makeshift cage. Ghoulish howls shook beams and baseboards, but despite his resistance, the Marquis of Hell was finally apprehended. Marchosias belched smoke and ash, glowing cinders rained from his snarling jaws, and he snapped his teeth at Colin before his body was pulled beneath the concrete. He clawed at the ground, leaving black welts across the floor in front of Colin's shoes, then he disappeared. The sound of him faded, and the smoke cleared, and Colin Hart felt his knees begin to buckle.

"Colin!"

Light ebbed at the corner of his vision. He turned toward Bishop, but before he could say a word—*are you all right, are you hurt, come here, Bishop*—consciousness snapped in half, leaving him swimming through blackness as he fell.

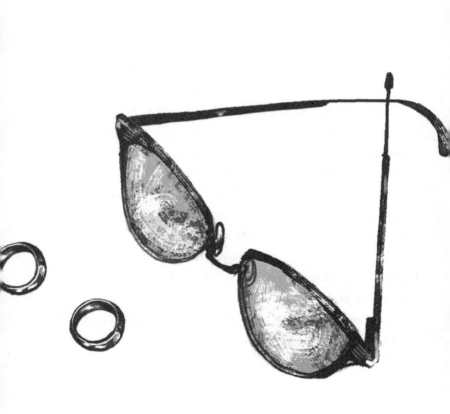

CHAPTER TWELVE

WHAT THE HELL ARE YOU doing here?

It's been five hours. Also, there's whole-ass corpse in your basement—sick shit, man. What's wrong with him?

He passed out—hey, wait!

Give it a rest, brujo. Okay, holy man, time to wake up—

Colin jolted awake. A pungent, acrid smell filled his nostrils and he jerked backward, fumbling to catch himself on his palms. He blinked. Gunnhild sat on her haunches between his legs, cleaning her face with her paws. He was thoughtless for a long moment. Empty except for the woozy feeling tipping around inside his skull.

Tehlor Nilsen tied a ribbon around a pouch of ammonia, mint, and lavender. "Welcome back," she said, and nudged her chin toward Lincoln's slouching corpse. "Who's that?"

"Give him a second," Bishop said. They crawled toward him and paused at his shins, tilting their head to assess his face, shoulders, chest, waist, face again. "You okay?"

My face. He mindlessly reached for the throbbing in his cheek and flinched. His fingertips came away sticky-red.

"My face," he said, repeating the first coherent thought that'd manifested. "I'm . . . I'm fine, I think. I just . . ." He swam through mind fog, clipping the edge of recent memories—strength, Marchosias, angel-speak, sinking inside himself, Isabelle's voice, Bishop calling his name, illicit power—and scratched Gunnhild between her ears with his unbloodied index finger. "It's quiet," he said, finally, and sighed, shifting his attention to Tehlor. "I didn't know people still used smelling salts."

"And I didn't know priests played Weekend at Bernie's with legitimate dead bodies," she said, barking out a laugh. Her rosy lips split into a grin. "Scratch that. I *suspected*; I just didn't actually believe it. Did you handle whatever mess was shackin' up in here?"

"I believe so," Colin said.

Bishop inched closer. "We need to clean that," they said, gesturing to his mangled cheek. They glanced at Tehlor over their shoulder. "How'd you even get inside . . . ?"

She arched a tapered brow and didn't answer.

"What time is it?" Colin asked.

"Late," Bishop said.

Tehlor snorted. "Almost four in the morning. Technically, early. Should I check on you two in another five hours? Make sure you're not passed out on the floor? Starting fights with baby deities? Falling prey to savvy ghosts?"

Colin hardly had the energy to frown.

Bishop rolled their eyes. "How 'bout I call you if we need you," they said sarcastically, and offered a thin smile. "But right now, I should fix his fuckin' face, okay?"

"Damn, okay," Tehlor said, scoffing. She extended her hand for Gunnhild and stood. Her upturned eyes transferred from Bishop to

Colin. She winked. Of course she did. "Good luck—bet that'll leave a badass scar."

"Wonderful," he murmured.

Tehlor offered a two-fingered wave. Her heeled boots clopped the staircase, footsteps hammering the floor as she crossed the house. The front door opened, closed.

Crisp, easy silence settled around them. Colin listened for held breath. Waited for energy to spike, temperature to drop, a voice to whisper from the shadow, but nothing moved. The house rested, finally. Gentled and relented and slackened. Colin stared at Bishop, at their buzzed head and strong nose, at their worried eyes and parted lips. Before he could lean forward and kiss them, they took his chin between their fingers and turned his head, leaning in to look at his wound.

Colin winced, wrinkling his nose. "Ouch, Bishop. Good heavens. *Easy.*"

"Hopefully butterfly stitches will hold," they said. They made the shape of Colin's exclaim but didn't repeat it. *Good heavens.* "What're we doing with him?" they asked. They tipped their head toward the ugly corpse in the uglier recliner.

"We'll put him in the wall," Colin said, entirely serious.

Bishop nodded and stood, offering their hand. "Yeah, okay," they said, as if he'd butchered the punch line on a poorly told joke. "C'mon, bandages and stuff are upstairs."

They didn't let go of his hand. He allowed them to tug him to his feet and guide him out of the basement. In the kitchen, they pushed on his shoulders, silently commanding him to sit on the table. He winced when they flipped the switch on the wall, illuminating the room, and tried to blink away the fog still spinning behind his eyes.

Colin Hart had been in many situations with many different people, but he'd never channeled other beings before. Never opened himself to be used, to be commanded. His bones were still reacquainting themselves with his body, blood still finding the right speed in his veins, ears still adjusting to the emptiness. He swallowed to wet his throat and studied Bishop's expression as they stepped between his knees and pressed a warm, damp cloth to his cheek.

His mouth tightened to suppress a flinch. "Are you all right?"

Bishop cupped his jaw with their free hand, angling him where they wanted. They didn't speak for a long time, just dabbed at the blood caked on his face, wrung the towel into a bowl, peered at his wound. After they'd brought the towel to his cheek three times and the water in the bowl swirled pink, they exhaled through their nose.

"You spoke a different language—one I've never heard before," they said, following the claw mark from the corner of Colin's eye to the underside of his jaw. "You . . . You became something else. I don't know how to explain it, I don't know if I *could* explain it—"

"I was able to channel the High Court. The voices you heard weren't mine, the things you saw weren't me. They were angels and saints, I believe. I'm not exactly sure if I could explain it either, but that's the best I can give you."

"I didn't know angels possessed people."

"They do. Much like their siblings, angels aren't very fond of us. They tolerate us, I think. Keep the balance, because otherwise this plane—this place—would empower their opposition."

"Did it hurt?"

"Not until it was over," Colin said. That might've been the first time he'd endured something without succumbing to the pain, to the terror of it. Except for Bishop, who he'd chewed over in his mind again and again, who he had no reason to continue orbiting, who would soon become another successful cleaning, another online re-view—*3.5 Stars: a little odd for an exorcist, tidy but irritating, engages in inappropriate and lewd activity when given the slightest opportunity, boring*—and might forget about him after he left. Because leaving was the next natural step. A handshake, a *thank you for your business*, a blank Christmas card signed with Colin's name and a tin of fudge popped in the mail on December 20th with the rest of his well-wishes to past clients. Extra fudge for Bishop, obviously. Maybe a phone call too. A text at least. *I still think of you.*

Bishop nodded. They touched their thumb to the sore skin beside the claw mark and tsked. It was the first time he'd heard them click their tongue like that, like a parent, like a worn-out lover.

"You should shower before I butterfly this," they said.

"Yeah, okay."

They took his hand again. On the stairs, their palms were clasped; down the hall, their palms were clasped; in Bishop's bedroom, their palms were clasped. They only let him go to twist the handle on their refurbished shower, freshly tiled in midnight black and fixed with silver accents. The claw-foot tub, surrounded by plants and candles, was adjacent to the toilet, facing a sleek vanity stocked with oils, perfumes, lotions, and a statue of the Virgin Mary.

Colin's mind still moved slowly. When Bishop tugged at the bottom of his sweater, he shrugged the garment off, and when they toed out of their socks and unzipped their pants, Colin thought, *Oh.*

The water ran hot. Scalded his shoulders and stung his cheek. He tipped his face into the spray and closed his eyes, leaning into Bishop's hand skating his vertebrae. He'd wanted this—exactly this—since he'd arrived at the house on Staghorn Way, but he was exhausted. Bone tired. Completely, utterly useless when it came to using his body for anything substantial. Bishop touched him carefully, though. Stepped under the water with him and let the blood crusted around their nostrils wash away. Sighed and gazed at Colin, eyelashes wet, skin flushed.

They soaped him; he soaped them. Lips grazed shoulders and collarbones, but that was all. Easy touches. Colin hadn't realized he would've begged for intimacy until right then. Would've crawled across hot coals, would've swallowed false sainthood, would've battled another Marquis of Hell, just for a chance at *this*. As the water lost its warmth, Colin mustered enough bravery to bump his nose against Bishop's temple and kiss the side of their head.

"I keep waiting to wake up," Bishop said.

Colin turned off the shower and handed them a towel off the rack. "Tomorrow might be jarring."

"What?"

"All this," he said, circling his hand in the air. "The quiet, the absence. Sometimes it's hard to get used to."

Bishop tended to his face. Crisscrossed clear tape over the gash on his cheek and pulled until the wound inched closed. He studied his reflection in the steamy mirror. A red line traveled from the corner of his eye to his jawline. Curved like a moon. The first scar he'd ever carried back from an exorcism. Bishop stood beside him, holding their towel at their navel. They looked incredibly soft—nipples smooth and ruddy, mouth set loosely, skin clean of any remaining blood.

"Stay here tonight," they said.

Colin had a hard time looking away from them. He nodded, though, and followed them into their bedroom.

Bishop closed the blinds and shook lavender oil into a diffuser on the nightstand. It spewed floral-scented vapor, curling like weak smoke toward the vaulted ceiling. The white sheets were chilly on Colin's bare skin, the comforter heavy over his chest. Headlights from a lone car snuck through the window and mottled the wall, and Colin fought to stay awake while Bishop climbed in beside him.

"Is it over?" they asked, so quietly Colin almost startled.

Ghost, he thought first, then, *no, only the haunted.*

"Yes, I think it is," he whispered. "I hope it is."

Bishop sighed. They turned onto their side and scooted backward, nudging themself against Colin. "Don't be rude," they mumbled, almost playfully.

Colin draped his arm around them, pressing his nose to their nape. "Sorry," he said, sighing against their neck.

The house quieted. Sleep came fast, like a snakebite, like a heartbeat, and Colin drifted off in the middle of a silent prayer.

The day came and went. Colin only stirred once, cracking his eyes open to find Bishop, awake and startled, blinking at him from the other side of the bed. Their pupils were blown, eyes glassy in the shaded room. He'd cupped their face, smoothed his thumb along their cheekbone, and hushed them like he would a child.

"It's me," he'd said, raspy and low.

They'd stuttered through a relieved breath and gone back to sleep.

The next time he woke, the bedroom had darkened as evening fell outside the window. He didn't know the time or how long the two of them had been asleep. Didn't know if hours or days had gone by. But Bishop was there, reaching for him, and Colin reached back.

They ghosted his wounded cheek and cradled the back of his head, bringing their mouth to his. Closed the space between their sleepy bodies, tucked their thigh along the inside of his leg and kissed him slowly. Thoroughly, with intent, with the purpose of *now* and *please*. The two of them were alone in the healing house, finally. Alone with each other.

Colin touched them reverently. He scooped his hand along their ribs and placed his thumb beneath their small breast, humming when they grasped his knuckles and fit his palm over their nipple, asking him to squeeze, sighing contentedly between his lips. Their fingers dusted his tattoos, trailing runes scattered across his torso, his arms, inked into the hollow of his hip. When he eased them onto their back, they went without protest, and when he touched them tenderly, they made weak, encouraging noises.

For a moment, Colin understood Bishop's need for rough, relentless sex, the desperate kind, lonesome and strangled by heartbreak, because making love felt heavier, somehow. Gentleness caused his chest to lurch. Looking at them, eyes half-lidded and lips trembling, made him want to stay in Gideon, Colorado at the house on Staghorn Way.

How terrifying.

When it ended, it didn't end. Bishop dug through the nightstand and found their strap, and everything started over. Them, straddling his waist, riding the silicone attached to his groin, breathing hard, unabashed, and extraordinarily free. Again, once more. Him, unmarred cheek pressed against white sheets, propped on his widened knees with Bishop's hand around his skull, holding him still, fucking him slow and deep. Time didn't seem to matter. He gripped comforter and skin, wrist and throat. Was held and handled, bitten and clutched to. After, once they were both limp and sated, Bishop tugged him into a steaming shower, and kissed him beneath the water.

The pair moved through the night together. Dressed together, cooked together—spaghetti, of course—dozed in the guest bedroom together, sipped tea together, and in the morning, when snow flurried past the windows and sunlight hid behind gray clouds, they wrapped Lincoln Stone in two thirty-nine-gallon trash bags and placed him in the basement wall together.

The concrete came away after a few swings from a sledgehammer. Dust puffed into the basement and Bishop swatted at the air.

They coughed, squinting behind their glasses. "I thought you were kidding about this."

"The house has been exorcised. This body has too. Keeping him here, bound to the place where he was cut away from demonism, prevents him from wandering back to you. You banished him, yeah, but you didn't *destroy* him. If the vessel is somewhere he can't return to, you'll be safe," Colin said.

"Fucking"—they smacked wet concrete onto a cinderblock and shoved it into place—"wonderful."

Colin doused the body in Holy Water and Bishop blew cleansing smoke into the thin pocket between drywall, foundation beams, and brick, then they pushed the last cinderblock into place and stuffed the cracks and creases with concrete and sealant. The wall would take hours—days, even—to dry completely, but Colin and Bishop pulled the linen shelf in front of the structural scar, and let it be. Bishop stood with their hands on their hips. Breathed shallowly. Stared at the space they'd stored Lincoln and kicked the floor with the toe of their boot.

"It's over," they said on a sigh.

Colin nodded. "Yeah," he said, and sighed too. "It's over."

He didn't want *this* to be over, though. Whatever the two of them had found together, whatever strange, wild thing they'd started. He wanted to keep it, to swallow it, to harvest it. He wanted Bishop Martínez.

"Do you have another job lined up?" they asked, uncertainly.

Surely, he might. If he checked his abandoned email, he'd find requests for consultations and inquiries from ghost-hunting squads. He could be on the road in hours.

"Not yet," he said, swallowing nervously. "I'll probably head to my next consultation in a couple days. Is it all right if I stay until I confirm with my next client? I can get a hotel if you—"

Bishop tripped into bright laughter. "Dios mío," they said under their breath, and shook their head. "You're insufferable, Colin Hart. You know that, right?"

He met their eyes, lips quirked into a sad smile. "I'm aware, yes."

"Stay." They brushed past him, swatting dirt off their palms, and took the stairs two at a time.

Colin glanced at the wall concealing Lincoln's body.

Bishop hollered, "Want a beer?" from the first floor.

He needed to control his heart, get his business in line, move on. He needed to figure out how to say *goodbye* to Bishop. How to get in his car and drive away. Colin needed to do a lot—too much.

But he said, "Yeah, sure." And met Bishop in the kitchen. Watched them blow on a naked candlewick and coax a flame to bloom, then kissed the magic from on their lips, and mouthed at their neck, and tasted dust and dirt and sweat on their supple skin. He thought, *God, give me strength,* when Bishop peeled his shirt away. Stole their beer and took a sip, yanking at their belt with his free hand. They made love on the floor, and fucked on the couch, and spoke sweetly to each other in front of the fireplace.

Show me how to let them go.

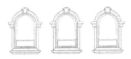

Dear Colin Hart,

I think my ex-wife is a witch. I'm pretty sure she cursed me after she found out about the affair—

DELETE

To Colin Hart,

Hi! We're a team of amateur spirit searchers on a quest to find PROOF of the afterlife! We'd love to set up an interview if you—

DELETE

Hello,

My name is Ginger Stockholm. My nineteen-year-old son killed our rabbit yesterday. He's always been a sweet boy. Very mild-mannered and soft-spoken. I'm sure you've heard stories of the unbelievable—according to your website, you're comfortable with handling these sort of things. I wish I was too. But Danny is getting worse. I don't know my own child anymore. I've done research. I know the signs. Insects, bodily changes, attitude shifts, animal slaughter, inhuman behavior. He killed our rabbit yesterday, and today we rushed him to the hospital to reattach his pinkie finger. He'd bitten it off. Flies have infested the garage, burning themselves to death on the light bulb because I refuse to turn it off. I'm a good Christian woman, Mr. Hart. I go to church, I read the gospel, I pray at the dinner table, but I am no exorcist.

And I believe I'm in need of one.

Colin read the email twice. He sat cross-legged on Bishop's bed while they groomed in the bathroom. The whir of the clippers filled the air and a bird chirped on the frozen windowsill.

Ginger Stockholm lived in Little Rock, Arkansas. If he left after dinner, he could drive through the night and make it to her house by tomorrow afternoon. His hands hovered over the keyboard, arguing with the rest of him. After a breath of hesitation, he typed and hit send. One minute later a response came through, bolded at the top of his inbox.

Dear Ginger,

I can schedule a consultation for tomorrow evening if you're still in the market for a specialist.

Best,

Colin Hart

Colin,

Yes. Don't be alarmed when you arrive. We've boarded the windows but we're home. Drive safely. Please hurry.

Blessings,

Ginger

He sighed through his nose.

"You look pensive," Bishop said. They stood in the doorway between the attached bathroom and the bedroom, scrubbing their palm over their freshly shaved head.

"Someone in Arkansas is dealing with a possession. It seems urgent," he said, pointing at his laptop.

"So you're leaving?"

"After dinner, yeah."

Bishop chewed their bottom lip and pulled at the webbing between their fingers. Their eyes flicked to the frosty window. "Should we order takeout?"

"We can," Colin said. The unspoken twisted between the two of them. Colin didn't want to leave, but he couldn't stay; Bishop didn't want him to go, but they couldn't ask him not to.

Since the moment Colin had arrived at the unstable house and met Bishop, they'd danced around each other. Found comfort in each other. Made something with each other. But the job was done, the house was clean, and Colin didn't know if their togetherness was a result of loneliness or grief or genuine compatibility.

It was all of those things, probably. Every single one.

"Does Thai sound good?" Bishop asked.

Colin nodded. He would've agreed with whatever they suggested, though. "Chicken Khao Soi with extra noodles, please."

Bishop's lips lifted into a crooked smile. They mouthed *okay*, unplugged their phone from the charger on the nightstand, and left the room.

Colin picked at the growing hole on his sock and tried to dismiss the sadness that'd cracked through Bishop's honey-brown eyes. He thought of last night, lying naked by the fireplace, telling stories to each other. *When I was a kid—at Christmas we—tell me about this one* as Bishop touched a tattoo. Thought of laughing against their neck while the two of them fumbled to undress each other. Thought of Bishop's fierce, ancient eyes lit by candlelight in the basement, their shadow prying magic from inside a living cadaver. Thought of holding their hand—of not holding their hand ever again—and swallowed around a childish lump growing in his throat.

He closed his laptop, slid off Bishop's bed, and walked into the guest bedroom to quietly pack. Folded his clothes and placed them in his rolling case. Slipped his laptop into his messenger bag, packed his toiletries, and stopped to stare at his reflection in the bathroom. The butterfly stitches holding his wound closed were stark against his freckled skin, reddish hair pushed away from his face, neck decorated with rosary beads and a small, circular hickey.

The doorbell rang. Colin startled. He exhaled slowly, blinking back the fight-or-flight this house had installed inside him over the last few days. Bishop thanked the delivery person, paper bags crinkled, and their voice flitted through the foyer.

"Food's here," they said.

Colin gave his room a once-over. Sheets, tucked. Pillows, fluffed. Carried his case downstairs and set it beside the door.

"Want a beer?" Bishop asked.

He shook his head and took his time walking into the kitchen, pressing the soles of his feet against the floor where they'd tangled together yesterday. "Coffee, if that's okay. I'll be driving for a while."

"Right. Obviously," they said, and filled the coffee maker with water.

Plates clinked, steam curled away from Colin's mug, and the silence deepened. Colin picked at his food, aware of Bishop's eyes on him, and when they turned toward their dinner, he lifted his gaze and knew they felt him watching too. It went on like that. Eating, looking, sipping, until the food was gone, and they were left with nothing but each other.

Colin met their eyes. He tried a weak attempt at a smile. Bishop did the same, curling their hands around their beer bottle while Colin finished his coffee.

"Weird bein' here without him," they said suddenly. "I know it shouldn't be. I should be okay with how . . . how the house feels without him wandering around, ghost or not, but . . . I don't know. He's never actually been *gone* before."

"Sometimes grief comes late," Colin said.

"Yeah, I've been grieving him for a long time, though. Too long."

"It's never predictable, you know. How a heart reacts to loss. I'll go three days without thinking about Isabelle, and on the fourth morning I'll smell her perfume at a café or hear her laughter in someone else's mouth, and I'll be catapulted back into the thick of it. I never know when it'll happen, I can never anticipate how it'll feel. Some days, I shake off the worst of it. Some days, I'll find a church to cry in. Some days, I drink. Every day is new, at least. I open my eyes and find a way to live without her."

Bishop nodded. They stared at the bottle, peeling the label with their thumbnail. "So how does this go, huh? *Keep in touch? Have a nice life?* How do you close a case, exorcist?"

Colin stilled. His throat cinched, but he breathed through the ache in his chest. Opened and closed his mouth, searching for something, anything.

"This isn't a typical case," he said, and it was the truth. "But I'd like to keep in touch if you're okay with that."

Their smile twitched and they adjusted their glasses. "Yeah, I'm okay with that."

"Good," Colin said. He knew what came next, yet he still hesitated.

"Good," they echoed.

Colin stood. He didn't know what to do with his hands, so he took his dish and mug to the sink, and he didn't know if he should leave abruptly, so he soaped the dirty plates and put them in the dishwasher. But after that, leaving was the only thing he had left to do. He cleared his throat and buttoned his coat, slung his messenger bag over his shoulder, and extended the handle on his hard-shell case.

"Text me and let me know you made it safely," Bishop said. They leaned against the banister with their arms folded across their chest and offered a barely-there smile.

He nodded because he didn't know what else to do. Because he wanted to kiss them, but if he kissed them, he'd stay, and he couldn't stay. Because Bishop Martínez was smart and brave and powerful and beautiful, and he did not want to leave. But if he didn't leave then, he might not leave at all.

So Colin Hart left. His polished shoes made hollow, hooflike sounds on the sturdy, renovated porch, and crunched on fallen snow. He threw himself into the driver's seat, closed the door, and locked it for good measure. But as he sat there, letting the engine purr, squeezing the steering wheel in a white-knuckled grip, he couldn't seem to put the car into *Drive* or place his foot on the pedal. He thought of his life without Isabelle, how terribly lonely it'd been, and tried his damndest to drive. *Just drive, Colin.* But he didn't—couldn't. He'd channeled angels and saints, ripped demons out of writhing bodies, captured ghosts and ghouls with his bare hands, but he couldn't leave Bishop without *trying.*

Truthfully, he hadn't realized he'd exited the car until he was trudging through the snow, stomping on the porch, and rapping his knuckles on the door.

Bishop answered while he was still knocking. "Colin, I—"

"No, wait—I'm sorry, I—I just think . . ." He paused to clear his throat. "I think you should come with me, actually. I mean, if you want to. There's no reason for you to be stuck in this house, and there's no reason to force-feed yourself grief, and there's no reason for me to live without you too. You're here—you're *right* here—you could just come with me . . . You could . . ." Halfway through his terribly ill-thought-out rambling, Bishop had started typing on their iPhone. Heat rushed to his face. "I could certainly use your help with this upcoming case, at least. We could . . . We could *try.* I don't know if it'll work, if we'll work, but we have worked—we've *been* working, us, whatever we are—and I just . . . I . . . Are you listening, Bishop? This is quite important—"

"I'm asking Tehlor if she'll water my plants while we're gone," they said, like someone would say *obviously*.

Colin blinked. His heart tumbled into his stomach. "Oh," he said stupidly. "Then you'll—"

Bishop shot him an impatient glance. They lifted one half-laced boot. "I was going to . . . to get you or stop you—*whatever*—but you came back before I . . ." They gestured impatiently to their shoes. "Let me get a bag."

"Well, pardon the inconvenience," Colin snapped, blushing furiously.

Bishop rolled their eyes and darted up the stairs. Drawers opened, closet doors banged, zippers pulled, and a few minutes later, they rounded the corner in the hall and loped back down the stairs, carrying a backpack and wearing their flannel coat. They locked the door with trembling hands and took long, brisk steps, ducking into the Subaru.

Colin had no idea what to make of this, of the two of them together, but he calmed his racing heart and fell into the driver's seat, staring ahead through the windshield with his brow furrowed.

"Are you sure?" he asked, blinking away surprise.

Bishop leaned across the center console and took his chin between their fingers, steering him into a kiss. They smiled against his mouth, sighing gently as he pitched himself closer, sinking into them, holding on to them.

"Drive, exorcist," they said.

Colin set his palm on Bishop's knee and watched the house on Staghorn Way, with its demons and its heartbreak, with its havoc and its mourning, disappear in the rearview mirror.

RETURN TO GIDEON

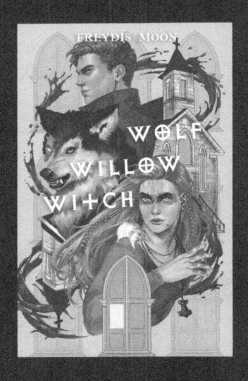

FREYDIS MOON

WOLF
WILLOW
WITCH

ACKNOWLEDGEMENTS

Heart, Haunt, Havoc is the result of sheer stubbornness, an inability to restrain myself, and the unstoppable will to breathe life into a terribly peculiar story. Truth be told, I thought I was the only one who would need this book, but then *Exodus 20:3* came into being, and *With A Vengeance* happened, and *Three Kings* made its way into the world, and I realized people like me would probably enjoy seeing people like us come together in a story filled with horror, tragedy, and resilience.

Thank you to my peers and mentors. Thank you to my readers for supporting my work. Thank you to the transgender creators who persevere in an opaque and daunting industry: you make work like mine feel possible and tangible, and your strength is contagious.

Thank you to my family, always. Thank you to the friends who adventure through life with me—cocktails in dimly lit bars, poetry in quiet cafés, music on long car rides, laughter in cozy kitchens—and choose to love me when I find it difficult to love myself. You keep me in my power when I can't seem to conjure it on my own. I am blessed to have you.

ABOUT ☽

Freydís Moon is a bestselling, award-winning author, tarot reader, and Pushcart Prize nominee. When they aren't writing or divining, Freydís is usually trying their hand at a recommended recipe, practicing a new language, or browsing their local bookstore. You can find their poetry, short stories, and fiction in many places, including *Strange Horizons*, *The Deadlands*, and elsewhere.

https://freydismoon.carrd.co

For information about the cover artist and interior illustrator, please find M.E. Morgan here: https://morlevart.com/

Made in United States
North Haven, CT
05 April 2024

50932475R00088